**Taking his hand, Imani pushed from the seat and lost her footing. Daman caught her by the elbow and pulled her into his embrace.**

After she regained her balance, she remained in his arms, mere inches from his face. His eyes ventured to her glossy pink lips. He'd never noticed how great lipgloss looked on a woman before. He wanted to kiss her lips until there was no shine left. There was nothing sexier than a thoroughly kissed woman, and he could imagine that Imani's lips looked even better after being kissed.

He felt her breath quicken as her eyes darted from his eyes to his mouth, as if mirroring his own thoughts. He wanted to kiss her, nibble on her lips. All he needed was one taste to feed his curiosity. He slowly eased her onto the desk to secure her balance. He kissed her neck, softly at first and then with a little tongue. She moaned in pleasure, grasping his head to keep him close. He didn't want to only kiss her neck, he wanted more....

**Books by Sherelle Green**

Harlequin Kimani Romance

*A Tempting Proposal*

---

## SHERELLE GREEN

has a dynamic imagination and a passion for reading and writing. As a young girl, she channeled her creativity and manifested her thoughts into short stories and poems. Although she loves to read all genres, romance holds a special place in her heart. Her love for romance developed in high school after stumbling across a hot and steamy Harlequin novel. She instantly became an avid romance reader and decided to pursue an education in English and journalism. Nothing satisfies her more than writing stories filled with compelling love affairs, multifaceted characters and intriguing relationships. A true romantic, she believes in predestined romances, love at first sight and fairy-tale endings. Sherelle is a Chicago native.

# A Tempting Proposal

## Sherelle Green

HARLEQUIN® KIMANI™ ROMANCE

To my grandmother Gladys, whose words of wisdom, language of encouragement and expressions of counsel inspired me to pen my thoughts for a book series. Your knowledge, faith and unconditional love reached out to the hearts of many.
You may be gone, but you're in my heart forever and always.
May you keep shining down on us from Heaven.

Recycling programs for this product may not exist in your area.

ISBN-13: 978-0-373-86309-9

A TEMPTING PROPOSAL

**HARLEQUIN**®
www.Harlequin.com

**Printed in U.S.A.**

Dear Reader,

Meet Imani Rayne and the proud owners of Elite Events, Incorporated. I enjoyed writing Imani and Daman's story. One of the key qualities I admire about Imani is her love and devotion to her family. While writing this fictional story, it was easy to reflect on the loss of my own grandmother—the inspiration behind Gamine. I have always been a firm believer in fate and predestined relationships. Through forces unbeknownst to them, Imani and Daman embark on the love of a lifetime and are able to let go of their pasts and embrace their future… *together.*

I hope you fall in love with Imani and Daman as I have. I'm currently working on the second and third installments in the Elite Events series. Cydney Rayne's story is next. I love to hear from readers, so please feel free to contact me.

Much love,

Sherelle

www.sherellegreen.com

sherellegreen@yahoo.com

@sherellegreen

To my loving and supportive family. You all are truly a blessing and I couldn't imagine my life without each and every one of you.

# Chapter 1

"This cannot seriously be happening," Imani mumbled as she tried to keep what was left of her patience. The speedometer in her gold Lexus hadn't gone over five miles per hour since she got stuck in this bumper-to-bumper traffic. Morning traffic in downtown Chicago was something she had never gotten used to. Her meeting with Mr. and Mrs. Sims was scheduled to begin any minute. She had thought she would make it in time if she left her condo two hours prior, but clearly she'd thought wrong.

The Simses owned several luxurious estates in Illinois and were founders of one of the best job-resource agencies in the country. Imani was meeting with them to discuss buying one of their top estates—the one that had the gorgeous view of Lake Michigan. She had promised her grandmother she would act fast when the Simses were ready to sell.

Imani's family and the Simses were close friends, and although many people were trying to get their hands on the estate, the couple had narrowed down the list of prospects to Imani and one other buyer. Unfortunately, the other buyer was willing to beat her price.

"Come on, move out of the way!"

Yelling alone didn't seem to get her point across, so she honked her horn for good measure. She didn't care what the other drivers thought of her. Her morning had begun badly when she'd realized her flat iron was broken, resulting in her having to straighten half her hair with a curling iron. The day became progressively worse after she spilled coffee on her favorite black business suit, and had to settle for a suit that fit her backside a tad tighter than she'd liked. The awful traffic wasn't helping matters. But just as she'd almost given up hope of ever making it off Lake Shore Drive, traffic finally started moving, and she reached her destination.

She entered the corporate building ten minutes late. "Hello. My name is Imani Rayne, and I have a 10:00 meeting with Mr. and Mrs. Sims."

The French receptionist waved her manicured hands toward two grand doors. "Mr. and Mrs. Sims are waiting for you. Please go right in."

Imani stepped into the conference room. "Hello, Mr. and Mrs. Sims. I'm so sorry I'm late." Imani gave a soft smile.

"No problem, sweetie." Mrs. Sims took Imani's hands in hers, stepped back and appraised her from head to toe. "Just look at you. It seems like just yesterday, you were a little baby girl holding your grandmother's pinkie finger. My, how you've grown."

As a teen, Imani felt like she'd never mature out of her awkward phase. She no longer had the look of an adolescent girl unaware of how to accentuate her curves and master her feminine walk. Now, she embraced her beauty and had confidence in her stride.

"We haven't seen you in so long, Imani. You seem to be doing fine, just a little sad in the eyes," Mr. Sims said.

"I'm fine. It gets a little easier every year. I still miss Gamine, but everything is going well."

It had been five years since her grandmother, Faith "Gamine" Burrstone, passed away. At times, she still felt the same gut-wrenching ache she felt that fateful day she'd gotten the news of her passing.

Mrs. Sims softly squeezed Imani's hand. "It takes time, and she wouldn't want you to be sad."

She gently stroked Mrs. Sims's hand. "I know."

"Let's get down to business," Mr. Sims suggested. He stepped aside to escort Imani to a nearby chair. Until that moment, Imani hadn't noticed the handsome gentleman with smooth chocolate skin sitting at the end of the conference table.

"Imani Rayne, I'd like to introduce you to Daman Barker, the other buyer vying for the estate."

Daman stood and walked toward her. "Ms. Rayne, it's a pleasure."

"Nice to meet you, Mr. Barker, but please call me Imani." She was surprised at how low and sexy her voice had gotten.

"It's nice to meet you, too, and you can call me Daman."

She grasped his hand a little longer than she should

have, surprised by the electric spark. The way his masculine hands encased hers shot shivers through every part of her body.

*Daman Barker is your competition. Pull yourself together, girl. You got this!*

Easier said than done. Daman was tall and muscular. And God bless the tailor who draped his body in that stylish, blue, pin-striped suit. The man had swagger. She'd noticed that much in his short stride from his seat to her side of the conference table. But that wasn't all she'd noticed. He was arrogant; she could tell by the way he carried himself. But goodness, he made arrogance look sexy.

She scanned her memory, trying to recall why his name seemed so familiar, but she came up short. He was observing her so closely that it was hard for her to keep her breathing under control. It felt like he could see right through her business suit. *Is he attracted to me, or is he just assessing his competition?* As if he knew her thought process, he winked and gave her a sexy smile, catching her off guard.

*Yes, it was definitely attraction.*

"Shall we get started?" Mr. Sims asked, interrupting the silent exchange between Imani and Daman.

"Yes," she and Daman both replied.

Mr. Sims tapped a small, disorderly bundle of paper on the desk until it lined up into a neat stack. "Okay, we have called you both here today because of your interest in our estate. We're having a difficult time making a decision. Therefore, we have a proposal for you both."

Imani sat and calmly glanced from Mr. Sims to Mrs. Sims. "And what would that be?"

"Well, you both are aware of the leading Black Enterprise Entrepreneurs Conference and Expo that takes place every year, allowing African-American entrepreneurs and business owners a chance to network and receive recognition for their work. I believe you both have members in your families that have been honored at previous conferences. This year, Black Enterprise is throwing the First Annual Performance and Achievement Awards Gala that will honor business owners and entrepreneurs on a much larger scale. Are you both aware of the gala?"

"Yes," Imani replied. Daman nodded his head in agreement.

Mr. Sims pushed back from the table just a bit, placing one long leg across the other and laying his hand over his ankle. "My wife and I are on the Black Enterprise executive board, and we were asked to choose event planners to organize the gala. We expect this event to be the premier destination event for business owners. It takes place on July 20th, three months from now, and requires the confirmation of approximately fifteen hundred guests, catering plans, pre- and post-party plans…the list goes on and on."

Imani looked at Daman. Since he appeared as confused as she felt, she asked the obvious question. "I'm sorry, Mr. Sims, but I don't follow. What does the gala have to do with our interest in the estate?"

Mrs. Sims smiled. "What my husband is trying to say to you both is that we've received approval from the board and would like to ask you both to plan the gala… together. Afterward, you two will decide who will get the estate. If you accept the challenge, we have numerous volunteers to help you."

Having numerous volunteers wasn't important to Imani. What was important was finding out why the Simses thought it was such a good idea for her and Daman to work together on this.

Mrs. Sims poured herself a glass of water from the carafe sitting near her side of the table. She took a quick sip before continuing. "I guess you should also know that last week we decided to sell one of our smaller estates. Although it isn't as exquisite as the estate with the lake view, it's definitely a beautiful property. Whoever does not get the lake-view estate will get the smaller estate."

Mr. Sims nodded his agreement. "We understand how you both must feel, and if you accept, the board will be happy to have you on the planning committee free of charge."

"Free of charge? Why wouldn't we get paid for this event?" Daman asked.

Mr. Sims smiled slightly before continuing. "As a consolation prize for your doing us this huge favor, we are willing to give those properties to you for a minimal fee." He handed Imani and Daman each a piece of paper detailing the prices for the estates.

"Why would you charge us so little?" Daman asked.

"Mr. Sims and I have made some very wise investments, so we have all the money we could ask for." Mrs. Sims softly touched her husband's arm. "This is something that we want to do, and we'd appreciate it if you took us up on our offer. Selling the estates was never about the money. It was more about ensuring that the estates were in very good hands."

Imani hated surprises, and she really wished the Simses would have taken her aside to explain their proposal before having the meeting. But as a friend of the Simses, she knew better than to debate them on the issue. "I need a day or two to think about this," she said.

"I do, too." Daman stood and moved toward Imani's chair. "Imani, I usually work in Detroit this time of year, but I will be in Chicago for a while. May I suggest that you and I talk about this over dinner tomorrow?"

Daman was right; they had a lot to discuss. But at the moment, she couldn't even think about the Simses' proposal because the man towering over her was making her heart skip a beat.

"Sounds like a plan," she said, satisfied that her voice wasn't as seductive as before. "Here's my card. Call me, and I'll meet you at the restaurant of your choice."

Daman nodded as he took the card in one hand and reached out his other hand, waiting for her to return the gesture. She hesitated outwardly, but inwardly she was certainly responding to him. She reached out her hand, lightly gripped his and was once again caught off guard by the magnetic spark she felt. The heat reflected in his eyes mirrored what she was feeling.

When she rose out of her seat, he let go of her hand but still stood close by. "Mr. and Mrs. Sims, it's been a pleasure. Imani and I should have an answer for you in, oh…" He looked Imani's way to allow her to say when.

"In a couple of days. As always, it was nice seeing you both," Imani said.

Mrs. Sims opened the door for them. "Imani, tell your family we send our love. We look forward to hearing from the two of you very soon."

## Chapter 2

Daman rocked his head to the beat of smooth jazz music as he sat in a popular downtown Chicago steakhouse, awaiting Imani's arrival. He'd called her earlier that day to settle on a location for them to meet and discuss the Simses' proposal. However, the business side of him had some strong apprehensions about accepting what they had offered. He knew there was a catch, but he didn't know what the older couple had up their sleeves. Regardless of his apprehensions, he knew he had to accept their offer and partner with Imani to plan the gala. He'd promised his father he would buy the property when Mr. and Mrs. Sims were ready to sell, and he couldn't disregard a promise. On his deathbed, his father told him that the estate would be the best investment he'd ever make. He also told him that it held answers to questions he didn't even know he had. Daman never got the chance to ask his father to expand on his request. So, Daman not only wanted the estate, he *needed* the estate. He knew there would be something there from his father. What it was, he wasn't sure.

Taking a sip of wine to calm his nerves, Daman pondered the proposal. He was anxious about his business dinner with Imani. This wasn't like him. He never got anxious about meeting with a woman. Then again, he had never gone months without sex, either. Dealing with pressing personal issues had recently forced him to put everything else on the back burner—even his physical needs. But meeting Imani ignited an inferno under that back burner.

Partnering with her wouldn't be the worst thing that could happen. He was irritated, though, at the way his body reacted to her. Even now he felt like he needed a cold shower. Maybe it was the way her body had sweetly filled out her business suit. Her luscious curves and fair golden-tan complexion were causing him a lot of discomfort. He'd closely assessed her when they were introduced, and the fact that she had boldly assessed him in return every time she caught his eye had made it hard for him to look away.

He glanced at his watch and took another sip of his wine just as he spotted her being escorted to his table. She walked like a woman on a mission.

"Daman, it's good to see you again," Imani said. She gave a soft smile but remained professional.

Any man could tell she was poised and she exuded confidence. He usually avoided overly confident women. In his experience, he found them to be too much work, even though his friends would say he never gave that type of woman a chance. On her, however, he had to admit that he liked the confident air.

He stood to pull out her chair. "Good to see you, too, Imani." The attraction was strong, and so was his anxiety. The faster they got down to discussing business, the better off his body would be.

"I'm sorry I'm a little late," Imani said as she took her seat. "My mom needed me to run an errand for her. Sometimes I think she's oblivious to how much work I do. But as she always says, 'A Burrstone's work is never done!'"

"No problem. I understand."

As she ordered her wine, he couldn't help but observe her natural beauty. Then a thought struck. "Hold on. You said Burrstone. I thought your last name was Rayne."

"Yes, it is. See, my mother is a Burrstone. My father's last name is Rayne."

"Oh, okay. By *Burrstone* you don't mean…" His voice trailed off. Imani was smiling a little too hard. Something about the way she smiled made him want to suck her lips and really give her something to smile about.

"If you were going to ask me if I was a Burrstone as in *the* Burrstones, then the answer is yes."

*Oh, so she's one of the infamous Burrstone women.* The Burrstone family was well-known across the county. Its members consisted of educators, business owners, famous actors and actresses, sports icons, politicians and entrepreneurs. They had founded several charities for children and less-fortunate families, and were highly involved in community events. They were greatly admired, and Daman had always liked the fact that they were a close-knit family.

It dawned on him to whom the Simses were referring when they spoke of the loss of Imani's grandmother during their meeting the other day. He remembered reading about her death a few years ago. From various articles and interviews, he knew that Faith or "Gamine"—as close family and friends affectionately called her—was a remarkable woman.

"I'm sorry about Mrs. Burrstone."

Imani grew quiet before speaking. "Thanks. I miss Gamine a lot, but I know she's in a better place."

"I know the feeling. I lost my father a while ago."

Daman wasn't sure why he had shared that information with her. He didn't share personal information about himself readily. He watched her trying to read his face and wanted to tell her to give up, since he wasn't an easy person to read.

"I know," she replied. "I did a little research on you before I got here. It must be hard for you. I couldn't imagine losing a parent."

Shrugging his shoulders, he blew off her words. The waiter stopped by their table, took their dinner orders and left again. After silent seconds ticked into minutes, Daman decided to get to the business at hand.

"So I've been thinking a lot about Mr. and Mrs. Sims's proposal and I don't think there's any harm in planning the gala and deciding who will get the estate."

"I agree," Imani replied. "I think good things can come out of planning the gala, and Mr. and Mrs. Sims have done more than their fair share for the community over the years. Have you ever planned an event this large before?"

"Yes. I've planned many client events and conferences for my company, Barker Architecture. I double majored in college so I have my bachelor's in both hospitality management and architecture. After college, I got my master's in business and marketing so I guess you can say I'm a jack of many trades."

"That's good to hear," Imani said.

"I heard you own an event-planning company, but rest assured I'll be able to handle my part of the planning," Daman added.

"So you've heard of me?" Imani asked, appearing impressed.

Daman had researched her after their initial meeting and clicked on the first link that popped up. He didn't know much, but the article he read was about her company.

"I heard a little something," Daman responded. "Then we have an understanding? We're planning the gala?"

"Yes, we have an understanding. But we need to decide how to split the duties, which days we have to go to Atlanta and who will go."

"I guess you didn't check your email?" Daman asked.

"No. Why, did you send me a message?" She reached for her iPhone and started scrolling through.

"Mr. and Mrs. Sims did. It's filled with information we would need to know just in case we decided to accept their proposal. We can change the schedule slightly, but not much. This is going to require a lot more effort than I thought, but I can adjust my schedule to manage it."

Daman pulled out a printed copy of the email and passed it to Imani.

He watched her expression as she glanced over the schedule. "There will hardly be any free time between work and organizing the gala." She seemed a little concerned.

Daman nodded in agreement. He liked the way her face wrinkled as she read the schedule. She didn't seem like the spontaneous type, so he figured the proposal threw her for a loop. He knew her type, and once you met one, you've met them all. Everything she did was probably calculated. He was the complete opposite. He lived for the moment and never thought too far in advance. He'd glanced at the schedule long enough to know a lot of work was ahead, but that was all.

"Imani, are you okay?" Daman asked. She had continued to look at the schedule even after they'd eaten the dinner that had been served.

She finally looked up from the paper after hearing Daman's voice. He could see the wheels in her brain turning.

"I'm sorry. It's just that if we have to follow this schedule, it seems we're going to be together a lot."

Her face became apprehensive. *Interesting.* "Do you have a problem being around me?" He smiled slyly. "I know I'm sexy and all, but I'm sure you can keep your hands off me long enough for us to plan the gala."

He didn't know why he was provoking her. It usually took longer for a woman to strike his interest enough for him to even participate in any type of banter. She was different from most women he dated…*not that this was a date,* he reminded himself. The more he flirted with her, the angrier she got, and he liked the effect he was having on her.

"By no means do you affect me, Daman Barker, and you won't distract me from my work. I'm going through with this proposal because I want my estate. I simply didn't know it required so much of my free time."

*Hmmm…she doesn't intimidate easily. I like that.* "By *my estate*, I hope you're talking about the smaller one."

Imani took another sip of her wine and adjusted the sleeves of her soft coral blouse. Leaning over the table, she stated in a clear voice, "No, I'm talking about the larger estate that you will agree to let me have after we plan this gala."

He laughed at Imani's bold statement. He had no intentions of letting her have the larger estate. "You know something, you seem very confident. Maybe too confident."

"I don't *seem* confident, Daman. I know the estate will be mine."

He winked at her and laughed when she rolled her eyes. He was sure she was usually very professional, but he was throwing her off her game. She obviously didn't like the look he was giving her, or probably any of the other looks he'd been giving her all evening.

"Daman, when I set my mind to something, I usually get what I want. And in this case, I want that estate, even if it means working long and excruciating hours with someone as arrogant as you."

It wasn't the first time he'd been called arrogant, and

it probably wouldn't be the last. He was only arrogant when backed into a corner. Imani hadn't done much, but he felt a growing need to push her buttons.

"You're clearly used to winning competitions. Well, I guarantee you that this is a competition you'll lose. Besides, you can't help that you're attracted to me. Most women are."

With a laugh, she looked him dead in the eye. "Daman, from what I've read about you on the internet, I know I'm not your type. Your name has been linked to the ditzy type—you know, women who can barely think for themselves. You're handsome and all, but you're definitely not my type. And I'm calling you on your crap because yesterday you were so into me that you could barely listen to the Simses. I saw it in your eyes—looking me up and down as if I were a plate of meat. You see me as a challenge, but trust me when I say that you can't handle a woman like me. So do us both a favor and get off your high horse."

He could hardly contain his smile at seeing Imani's look of satisfaction. She was right about one thing. Even today, she looked good enough to eat. But he refused to let her get the upper hand.

"You're right. At one point you had my complete attention yesterday." He dropped his voice even lower before continuing. "But it's only fair that I call you on your crap, too. You're attracted to me. You know it. I know it. I'm sure Mr. and Mrs. Sims know it. The difference is that you are playing with fire, Imani. You're definitely not too much for me to handle and I'm not afraid to act on the attraction. No matter how confident you seem today, I remember how our chemistry caught you off guard before. If you want to play this game, then be prepared to be eating out of my hands. I'm good at what I do."

He was forgetting his manners, and for a minute, he regretted what he'd said because he knew it could be taken more than one way. Then he remembered that anything he could do to throw her off her game was a plus, since he really needed to get the estate.

"Well, I have to go," Imani said, clearly appalled by his egotistical comments. But like the pro he could tell she was, she quickly recovered and continued their conversation. "I'll be busy rearranging my schedule, so it won't conflict with planning the gala. How about we meet Friday?"

Daman needed to make arrangements at work, too. "I'll call you and work out the details for Friday."

Imani stood to leave and placed the schedule in her purse. "I look forward to it. And hopefully, you'll check your arrogance at the door next time we meet," she stated in a sharp tone.

As Daman watched her walk out of the restaurant, he couldn't help but admire how gracefully her juicy behind swayed in her suit. *Her thickness should not be hidden under clothes.*

When he'd promised his father he would buy the estate with the lake view when the Simses were ready to sell, he didn't think he'd be going up against such a beautiful woman. He settled the check and left the restaurant, knowing his body wouldn't let him get any sleep tonight.

# Chapter 3

"So Mr. and Mrs. Sims want you to plan one of the biggest galas of the year with one of the most sought-after bachelors in Detroit?" Mya Winters, one of Imani's business partners and best friends walked into Imani's office and sat in a chair near the desk. At twenty-nine, they were proud owners of Elite Events Incorporated, along with Imani's twenty-seven-year-old sister, Cydney Rayne, and cousin, Lexus Turner.

"You know Daman Barker?" Imani asked as she poured herself a cup of coffee.

"I've heard his name around."

"And we've seen a picture or two," Cyd added, as she and Lex walked into Imani's office and took a seat on her sofa. "We also presented him with an offer to be featured in the most-eligible bachelors' edition of our magazine in a few months. Didn't you read the documents I placed on your desk?"

"No, I didn't. Sorry."

"That's okay. I know you've been busy."

Truthfully, they'd all been busy, and Imani wished she hadn't taken on so many additional projects. Although each woman ran their respective divisions, Imani knew that she sometimes took on more than she could handle in her own division. The same could be said for her involvement with her family.

"So what are you going to do?" Lex asked the question, but all three women appeared to be listening intently.

"I told the Simses and Daman that I accepted the proposal, but I don't like feeling obligated to work with anyone. Regardless, I know I need to suck it up and play nice. Although Gamine never told me why she needed me to purchase the estate, she did say it would hold the answers I've been searching for. The estate is finally in my reach to purchase, and I've been waiting five years to see what answers may lie inside. Whether it be a box or a letter, I need to know."

The look between Cyd and Lex didn't go unseen by Imani so she decided to divert from talking about Gamine.

"Plus, my initial meeting with Daman didn't go so well."

"Why not?" Mya asked.

"He's arrogant, cocky and thinks he's God's gift to women."

"Seems like most of the men we know," Mya said with a laugh.

"That may be true, but something about him gets under my skin. If last night was any indication of how working with him will be, then I need to really think about this."

"Hmmm…usually you're so good with words that even the cocky guys eventually quit with that nonsense," Cyd stated. "Could it be that your attraction to him is what's really aggravating you?"

Imani looked at Cyd in disbelief. "What makes you think I'm attracted to him?"

"Oh, come on, girl," Mya chimed in. "We've all seen his picture. Daman's your type. Simple as that."

Imani sighed as she stood and glanced out her office window before turning her attention back toward the women. "That's the other problem. When the Simses first introduced us, the attraction between us was obvious, and you all know my policy about fraternizing with men I work with."

The three women shook their heads at Imani's comment.

"You can't constantly work hard and never allow yourself time to relax," Lex said. "I can't even remember the last time you were attracted to a man."

"That's because I don't have time for them."

Cyd walked over to Imani. "Last time I checked, you didn't need a lot of time to enjoy a man's company. Plus," Cyd continued while nudging Imani's shoulder, "you and Daman will only be partners for a short time."

"I know, but I need to stay focused. No one thought that four women as young as us could have built such a successful company so fast. That's part of why you all don't date, either, because deep down we know men equal trouble. And trouble makes us lose focus of our goals."

"I disagree," Mya said. "At least *we* choose to date every now and then. But you haven't let loose in a while, which is crazy considering how you used to be. Don't you miss it?"

Imani glanced up at her friends and business partners because she knew there were words left unspoken. Since Gamine's death, Imani was far from the person she once was. She used to be more carefree and had no problem enjoying a man's company or living in the moment. Gamine had always encouraged her to follow her dreams and start her own event-planning business. The fact that her best friend since college, sister and cousin all shared a similar dream was a huge plus. Each of them had talents in different areas, and their business took off like wildfire. Besides being founders of a successful business, they also owned several Boys & Girls Clubs and published their own bimonthly magazine. Each alternated as head planner per event and actively managed a different part of the company. Imani's focus was on business management and sales; Cyd did marketing and advertising; Lex handled communications and public relations, and Mya worked on educational training and sponsorships. They were a force to be reckoned with, each having accomplished so much before the age of thirty.

Coming out of her trance, Imani noticed that they were still waiting on her response to Mya's question.

"Yes, I do miss having male company, and you're right, I haven't let loose in a while. I know it's time for me to try to make some changes to get out of this funk I'm in, but unfortunately, that's easier said than done." Sitting down at her desk, she took a sip of her coffee, thinking she'd added just enough cream to make her coffee almost the exact color of Daman's velvety, chocolate skin.

"Enough with all the serious talk," Cyd said in an attempt to lighten the mood. "Let's get down to the real business. Just how sexy is Daman in person?"

Imani shook her head as she thought about the right way to describe her first encounter with Daman. "Honestly, besides being arrogant and cocky, all I can tell is that he's confident and successful."

"Seriously?" Cyd asked, with a look of disbelief. "That's all you got?"

Imani exhaled. "No, that's not all. He's also tall, nicely groomed and has smooth, chocolate skin, which I definitely like. His eyes remind me of dark chestnuts and his smile is so sexy. And goodness, what a body. If you could have seen how he looked in that suit…" Her voice trailed off when she noticed how quiet her friends were. The knowing looks on their faces proved that she'd said too much already.

"But that won't change anything," she quickly added.

All the women laughed. "Oh, yes, it will," Lex said. "There is only so much a woman can handle. You've always been a sucker for Daman's type, so I don't see why this situation will be any different."

"Lex has a point. The sooner you admit that we're right, the easier he will be for you to handle," Mya added. "We already know how the corporate world works and Daman wants the estate, too, so he'll pull out all the stops to get it. You don't need to suck it up and play nice. You need to get your head in the game and go out balls blazing. The two most important things are to help plan one of the biggest events that Elite Events has ever been a part of *and* win the estate."

"You're right," Imani replied, allowing Mya's positive energy to rub off on her. "Organizing such a grand event will be amazing and beneficial. Besides, I can work on convincing Daman that I should get the lakeview estate. Y'all know how convincing I can be when I want something."

"Hell, yeah! Now you need to keep that attitude," Cyd stated.

"And pull out all the tricks because you know he will, too," Mya added.

"Cyd and Mya are right. But please don't stress about your attraction to Daman," Lex said with a smile.

Imani wondered if there was anything they didn't know about her. She was still apprehensive because she usually liked to plan ahead before diving into things, but she would never have turned down such an important proposal as the one from Mr. and Mrs. Sims.

"You're all right," Imani replied.

"Then it's settled?" Mya asked. "You already said yes to the Simses' proposal. Give Daman a run for his money. Even if that means seducing him, like he probably will try to do to you."

The situation really didn't seem settled at all, but Imani always prided herself on seeing the bright side. Fidgeting with the nameplate on her desk, she tried to hide her apprehension. But she never backed down from a challenge, and Daman Barker was definitely a challenge. "Yes, it's settled." *Let the games begin!*

# Chapter 4

When Daman walked into R&W Marketing Tuesday morning, he immediately felt at ease. Every time he walked into the firm that his boys, Taheim Reed and Jaleen Walker, had successfully established, he felt a sense of accomplishment. Two months ago, he decided to partner with his best friends full time to bring R&W to the next level. If Taheim and Jaleen could run a successful business and also be junior partners in their family businesses, he didn't see any reason why he couldn't, too. Daman had been traveling between his Detroit hometown and the windy city of Chicago almost every week by plane or car, but planned on making Chicago his permanent home by the end of the year. At thirty, he was proud of what he'd accomplished so far. Although Daman's career was thriving with R&W, he couldn't say the same for his feelings about Barker Architecture.

His father, Stan, and uncle Frank had opened Barker Architecture when they were in their early twenties. Now, Barker Architecture had grown to an astounding fifteen offices. They were responsible for much of the beautiful architecture and amazing landmarks throughout the Midwest. When Daman's father passed away eight years ago, his uncle took over as president and chief executive officer of the company. His uncle had never had children of his own, so he treated Daman like the son he never had. Daman had just graduated from college and was working on his master's, but his uncle picked up where Daman's father had left off and began showing him all the ins and outs of the company. When Daman became vice president of Barker Architecture, he began noticing inconsistencies with some of the accounting documentation. Barker Architecture was one of the companies affected by the 2008 economic crisis.

In order to keep the company afloat, Barker Architecture reached out to several investors, many of whom were old friends of Daman's father. When Daman became vice president in 2011, he wanted to focus all his energy into ensuring Barker Architecture would never be a victim of another economic crisis, so he began looking into the company's accounting files. His uncle was quick to try and divert Daman away from his personal investigation, but Daman continued to question his uncle about certain accounts and customers. Was Barker Architecture really in trouble in 2008? Or was his uncle hiding something? A few months ago, Daman decided it was finally time for him to step away from the office to figure out what was really going on. Since their second largest office was in Chicago, Daman told his uncle he would work out of that office and return to Detroit weekly or biweekly as needed. His uncle agreed, considering he was also aware of Daman's new partnership with R&W.

As Daman walked into R&W, he tried to put Barker Architecture out of his mind for the moment, but a phone call earlier that morning had been filled with disappointing news concerning just that.

"Hello, Mr. Barker!" the perky front-desk receptionist said, breaking his thoughts.

"Hi, Sherry. Are there any messages for me?"

Flipping her auburn hair behind her ear, she shuffled through a stack of papers. "Yes, you have several. Mr. Kingsberg called to recap last week's meeting, and Mrs. Remmy called about her upcoming meeting. Also, Glamour Cosmetics, Franko Industries and William's Whole Foods are all interested in starting an account with R&W. Mr. Reed and Mr. Walker would like you to begin working on those accounts."

"Thanks, Sherry."

"You're welcome, Mr. Barker." She snapped her fingers. "Oh, and I almost forgot! Imani Rayne from Elite Events Incorporated called your connected line and asked if you could call her back when you got a chance."

Daman smiled. He'd wondered if she would call. His connected line was the private line displayed on his business card for Barker Architecture. That was the only line connected to both Barker Architecture and R&W Marketing.

"Is that all she said?"

"Yes, Mr. Barker. She left her work number for you to call back."

"Thanks again, Sherry."

Daman looked at the clock sitting on Sherry's desk to see how much time he had before his meeting with Taheim and Jaleen. Noticing he only had three minutes to spare, he placed the paper displaying his messages in his suit jacket and headed down the hall.

He walked into the large conference room and was immediately greeted by both men.

Taheim was the first to speak. "Man, Jaleen told me about the proposal to plan the gala. That would be great exposure for R&W. You agreed, right?"

"Of course."

"Great. Did you decide when you want to announce your partnership with R&W?"

"I'm not sure, exactly. I'm still trying to tie up a few things at Barker Architecture before making the announcement, but I will definitely do it before the gala."

Taheim and Jaleen nodded in agreement.

"Who are you planning the gala with?" Jaleen asked. "I don't remember you telling me on the phone the other day."

Daman wished he'd been able to stop thinking about Imani.

"A woman, and a very attractive woman at that. We didn't get off to the best start. She thinks I'm arrogant and cocky. But you know me. I'm determined to show her my softer side." He gave his best "all-American boy" look and placed his hands over his heart in exaggeration.

Taheim laughed. "Already on the prowl, huh?"

"Well, yeah, but there's something about her. She's

educated, successful and confident, and I know she wants the gala to be a success, too."

"D, no offense, but the women you mess with are never educated, successful, or confident. Well, a couple have been, but not many."

"I know. She's different."

"What's her name?" Jaleen asked.

"Imani Rayne." No sooner than her name left his mouth, did Taheim spill his coffee on the table.

"Is everything okay, man?" Daman asked.

Taheim and Jaleen shared a look that didn't go unseen by Daman. Taheim cleaned up the spilled coffee.

"Yeah, man. I'm good. Have the two of you met yet?"

Daman didn't like not knowing what was up with his boys. He tried to squash the tinge of jealousy he felt. "Yeah, we met. Why? Did one of you date her or something?"

"No," both men replied in unison. They didn't date each other's exes, and he didn't even know why he cared. It's not like he wanted to date her. Daman Barker didn't date; he entertained.

Jaleen began to speak, but he was cut off by Taheim.

"The truth is that we've heard of her and her family. Not much happens in Chicago that her family isn't involved with socially or politically."

Jaleen nodded in agreement. "Not to mention she's attractive, and so are all the women in her circle."

Daman felt like there was more to the story than either man was telling him, but he chose to ignore it.

"Okay, well, she called me about the gala, and I was

going to return her call right after this meeting. Could we talk more after I finish the call?"

"Sure, man. We'll talk at lunch or something."

Daman walked into his tastefully decorated office, sat down at his desk and began dialing the number Imani had left in her message.

"Thank you for calling Elite Events Incorporated. How may I direct your call?"

"Hello. May I please speak with Imani Rayne?"

"May I ask who's calling?"

"Daman Barker."

"One moment, Mr. Barker."

Daman enjoyed the upbeat R&B music that played in the background. It was much better than the dreadful elevator music most companies played when they put you on hold.

Imani's voice suddenly filled the line. "Hello, Daman. Thanks for returning my call so promptly."

"You're welcome. I assume your call has something to do with the gala?"*Although I wouldn't mind if it were about something more personal.*

"Yes. I was wondering if we could meet tomorrow instead of Friday to discuss the plans. I'm going to make an appearance in Atlanta next week. So I figured I could introduce myself to the team when I get there."

"Okay, that sounds good. One of us should go to make sure we know the people we're working with. Where do you want to meet?"

"How about 6:00 p.m. at my place?"

Daman was shocked. After dinner the other day,

he figured most of their meetings would be in public places. "Your place?"

"Yes, my place. Is that okay with you?"

"Oh, yeah, that's fine. I'll be there. What's your address?"

After Daman hung up the phone, he thought about what tomorrow had in store. He knew Imani would try her best to remain collected around him, but he enjoyed making her nervous. She probably thought she hid it well, but she didn't. He would use their mutual attraction to his advantage, and persuade her to give him the estate. One thing was on his side: women could be just as cutthroat as men, but they had more difficulty separating business from pleasure. Daman knew better. He played the game with his mind. Emotions only stood in the way and made you lose touch with reality. A woman didn't stand a chance against a determined man, and after only two meetings, seducing Imani was at the top of his to-do list.

# Chapter 5

Imani spent a full two hours trying to get ready for her meeting with Daman. She didn't know why she was making such a big deal about seeing him. She kept reminding herself that it was strictly business and to ignore the discomfort she always felt in his presence. He was due to arrive in ten minutes, and she still felt mentally unprepared for his visit. She looked at herself in the mirror for the twentieth time.

*Man, I look good!* She had chosen to dress casually. A clingy mahogany maxi dress softly hugged her curves and complemented her flawless complexion. The dress was sure to make his mouth water, putting her at a great advantage.

The buzzer to the condo's security desk rang.

"Yes, Bernard?"

"There's a Mr. Barker here to see you."

"Thank you, Bernard. Please send him up."

With one more glance in the mirror, Imani took a deep breath and made her way to the door. *Here goes nothing....* Opening her door, she was greeted by Daman's seductive smile.

"Hello, Imani. Nice to see you again."

"Likewise, Daman. Please come in."

As he made his way into her condo, she heard him take a deep breath. His eyes were burning a hole in her dress, causing her stomach to flutter. She moved to the couch and bent over, pretending to fluff the pillows as she motioned for him to take a seat. She was fully aware that he was watching her every move. She knew what she was doing, and even though this was only their third meeting, she could tell he appreciated a woman with a nice butt.

"Did you get here all right?"

Daman cleared his throat before answering. "Yes, your building was easy to find."

"Great. Would you like anything to drink?"

"Yes, a Coke would be fine."

"Coming right up."

Imani made her way to the kitchen, making sure she swayed extra hard while she had his undivided attention. She heard him mumble something under his breath that sounded a lot like *damn*. She had to admit, he definitely looked handsome in his blue sweater and dark jeans, but she felt a sense of power in seeing his reaction to her seductive dress.

"One point for me," she said to herself when she reached the kitchen, licking the tip of her finger and swiping an imaginary number one in the air.

When she returned, she noticed her short trip to

the kitchen had allowed Daman enough time to regain his cool.

"Here you go." She handed Daman his drink. "Shall we get down to business?"

"Yes. When are you leaving for Atlanta?"

"I'm leaving this Friday, but I'm only staying over the weekend. I'll work with the gala volunteers over the weekend. Then I have to be back in Chicago because I'm interviewing on *The Jimmy King Morning Show* on Z105."

Imani sat on the couch a little closer to Daman than she had originally planned.

"That sounds great," Daman responded, taking a sip of his drink.

She watched the movement of his Adam's apple as the liquid slid down his throat.

Imani shifted to adjust her dress, aware that Daman's eyes had now ventured to her breasts. She perked them outward, glad she'd worn her new Victoria's Secret push-up bra.

"I met Jimmy King at a party we planned for Jennifer Hudson a couple months ago, so originally I was going on his show to advertise and discuss Elite Events. Now, I'm going to discuss the gala, as well. I've talked to the Simses and it's been approved for me to discuss the event."

"I'm sure you'll do well," Daman said with a smile. "So are you proud of everything Elite Events has accomplished so far?"

"Of course I am. Nothing beats going into business for yourself. What about you? How do you like being the vice president of Barker Architecture?"

She noticed the slight tightening of his jawline before he told her that he enjoyed it. Sensing he was uncomfortable with the subject, she decided to let it go—for now.

"Okay, so I figure the first thing I'll do the morning after I check in to my hotel is head down to the location of the gala. I have a contact list that Mrs. Sims emailed me, so I'll make a few calls and see who can meet me there."

"Sounds good. Be sure to see if the volunteers are as excited about helping as Mr. and Mrs. Sims made it seem. What's next?"

"Well, I think we should start with the guest list. I have no idea exactly how many people have RSVP'd, so I'll need to talk to Vicky Gordon, the head volunteer. I was under the impression that catering, decorations and media are all in the works, but nothing is finalized."

"Same here. Mr. Sims emailed me with strict instructions for both of us. The issue that seems to need immediate attention is the media. The same news shows and television stations that always televise and broadcast the gala will be there. However, we need to make sure that we still maintain a certain amount of privacy for our guests during all the pre-gala events. We want everyone to be comfortable."

"Yes, we do. I have some contacts in the media that I can reach out to. I think I emailed so many questions to Mrs. Sims that she decided to send me a really detailed to-do list. This list covers more of what we need to do for the pre-gala events."

Imani handed Daman the list, and her hand briefly grazed his. At the previous dinner, they hadn't had any physical contact, making this only the third time they'd touched. She couldn't help but enjoy how stimulating the sensation was. The glazed look in Daman's eyes told her that he had felt it, too. She couldn't help but wonder what sensations other body parts could create if she almost melted by the light touch of his hands.

They spent the next two hours discussing Imani's list of things to do and calling volunteers. Much to Imani's surprise, most of the meeting remained professional.

"Imani, I must say it was a pleasure discussing business with you."

"It was surprisingly a pleasure for me, also," she replied with a sly look on her face.

Daman liked the look Imani gave whenever she was being sarcastic, yet flirty. He just laughed at her comment.

"I'll give you an update on the gala when I return next weekend."

"Great. I look forward to it." As Daman began walking toward the door, he saw something flicker out of the corner of his eye. He looked in that direction and noticed a gold frame on the fireplace mantel that caught the light. For some reason, he needed to get a closer look at the photo in the frame.

Daman could tell that Imani was wondering what had caught his attention. He walked over to the photograph and studied the picture with intense concentration.

"Daman, is everything okay?" Imani asked, breaking his concentration.

He couldn't explain why he kept staring at the photo. The little girl in the picture was undoubtedly Imani. Her facial structure and features looked the same now as they did when the photo was taken, only more mature. Yet there was a slight difference he couldn't place that had nothing to do with maturity.

"I'm fine. Who's the woman in the picture with you?"

Imani walked over to her fireplace. "It's Gamine." She picked up the photo and lightly touched the frame. "It was taken when I was seven. Gamine had taken me out of town on a shopping trip. We had the best time."

Daman knew Imani and Gamine were extremely close, so it was hard to see her look so lost as she stared at the photo. Imani set the frame back down and quickly glanced at him before her eyes settled back on the photo. In that short second, he saw the flicker of despair in her eyes.

*That's what it is.* Imani's eyes had noticeably changed since her youth. In the photo, her eyes were filled with love and happiness, yet in the few times Daman had seen her, they lacked the same elation that the photo captured. She had been a carefree child, and she now carried the weight of adulthood on her shoulders, but his inner voice told him it was something deeper than that.

Imani abruptly stepped back from the fireplace. "Shall I walk you out?"

Her voice sounded pleasant enough, but she wore a plastered smile on her face that might have appeared genuine to many. Daman knew the difference, but luckily for Imani, he wasn't the type to interfere in other people's business. He didn't even know why he cared so much, and the fact that he was so curious about how she felt worried him. He decided it was best if he left before he did or said something he would regret.

"Thanks for a good evening, Imani. Have a safe flight, and feel free to call me if you need anything while you're in Atlanta."

"Thanks, Daman. Have a good weekend."

After the door closed behind him, Daman tried to process his reaction to the photo. "What is it with this woman?" he asked to no one in particular before heading home.

# Chapter 6

As Daman walked toward his private jet at the Chicago Aurora Municipal Airport, he massaged the back of his neck, trying to work out the knot that had developed. He didn't know if the cause of his discomfort was due to all the commuting between Detroit and Chicago, or to the couple in the hotel room next to his who'd constantly argued until 3:00 a.m.

Yesterday, he'd called his friend Thompson Davis, better known as "Tommy" on *The Jimmy King Morning Show,* to see if he could be a surprise guest the same day Imani would be on the show. Daman was honest with Tommy, knowing that he would jump at the chance to pull something unexpected on the show. He wasn't surprised when Tommy agreed.

He didn't tell Imani he was going to be on the show and he couldn't wait to see the look on Imani's face when she realized he would be in Atlanta at the same time she was. After the night they'd met at her place, after that dress she'd worn to purposely throw him off his game, he knew he had to regain some ground. And keeping his appearance on the show a secret might help give him a leg up. He needed to throw her off balance, and he suspected she hated surprises.

Reaching for his phone, he quickly dialed his mom. He and his mother were extremely close. His parents had experienced several miscarriages early in their marriage, but then on his mom's thirty-eighth birthday, she'd gotten pregnant with him.

"Good morning, Mom! How are you?"

Patricia Barker yawned softly. "Daman, baby, it's 5:00 a.m. I love hearing from you, but why are you calling me so early?"

He laughed at his mom's comment. "I thought you'd be up already."

"Daman, I'm an old retired woman. I don't need to get up at the crack of dawn—especially on a Monday."

"I just wanted to let you know that I'm leaving for Atlanta in a few minutes. The jet is waiting now."

"Is this for the gala?"

"Yes, it is. I'll be in Atlanta with my partner this week. Then I was thinking about dropping by to see you."

"I would love that, baby. I've been waiting for you to come down here."

"I know, Mom. My visit is long overdue." Daman had not been by to see his mom since she moved to Florida two years ago. She usually visited him in Detroit.

After a few more minutes, he ended the conversation and boarded the jet.

He would be at his destination shortly, so there was no time for a nap. He had to make a quick stop in Detroit before going to Atlanta.

Daman composed himself as he exited his jet and walked toward his rental car. The meeting he was about to have would, no doubt, impact his life. Regardless of the outcome, he needed to figure out what was going on with his uncle.

He pulled into the secluded parking lot of a forest preserve for his meeting with Private Investigator Malik Madden.

"It's good to see you again, Malik," Daman said.

"Same here. Shall we get right down to it?"

"Yes. My uncle has been very good about covering his tracks. I'm hoping you'll be able to provide me with enough evidence to bring him down once and for all."

Malik looked at him with concerned eyes. "Daman, I appreciate your confidence in me, and you're right, I am very good at what I do. If your uncle is keeping any secrets, I'll find out, but you have to be prepared for all outcomes."

"I understand completely. The pros outweigh the cons. For the past few years, I've watched my uncle carefully and something isn't right. I need to find out what he's got up his sleeve. It's about time I stand up for my father's dream." Daman understood Malik's concerns, but he knew this was the right thing to do. He was sure Malik had seen many people back out of investigations that turned ugly. But Daman would stop at nothing to reach his goal.

"I will contact you periodically as needed." Malik handed Daman a large manila envelope.

"Here is an outline of your case. Everything you need to know or do is explained in this envelope. Like you said, your uncle did a very good job of covering his tracks."

"Right," Daman agreed. "And my father was a great businessman. The company was extremely prosperous when he was alive. It's hard to believe that Barker Architecture wouldn't have had enough funds to stay afloat."

"I understand your concern and sooner or later we will figure out what your uncle's hiding," Malik replied.

Daman took the folder from Malik, hoping the case would get cracked sooner rather than later.

Imani eased into the luxurious hotel bathtub just as her iPhone rang. "Hello?"

"Hi, sweetheart. How was your flight?" Hope's happy voice floated through the phone.

"Mom, I'm so glad it's you! It was fine. How's Fiji?"

"Oh, baby, Fiji is wonderful. Your father and I just spent all day on an amazing tour of the island."

"That's great, Mom."

Imani grinned as her mom told her about the trip so far. She was happy for her parents, especially her mom. She had taken Gamine's death the worst of all, yet she was finally returning to her old self.

"I'm happy for you and Dad. You two needed a vacation. And you seem happy."

Imani hoped her mom hadn't heard the slight break in her voice.

"Baby, you have to get out of this funk you've been in. Ever since Gamine's death, you've been like the Energizer bunny, making sure everyone else is okay. I'm worried that you're not taking care of yourself."

Her mother was right. She couldn't explain how she felt and knew that her mother would see through her lie if she told her she was fine.

"I know, Mom. I want you to enjoy the rest of your vacation. When will you get back to the States?"

"Your father and I are thinking about extending our vacation and going somewhere else after Fiji. But we'll make sure we get back before the family barbecue."

"Wow, I'm jealous," Imani said with a laugh. "Retirement suits you both really well. I love you, Mom. Tell Dad I love him, too, and I'll talk to you both later."

"Okay, sweetie. I love you."

Hope hung up with her daughter and sighed deeply.

"Is everything okay with Imani?"

She turned to her husband, who still looked every bit of sexy at his age.

"I guess she's fine. I just wish I could help her out of this dismal mood she's been in lately. I know Gamine's death was hard on all of us, but Imani has always been the emotional and nurturing one…just like Gamine. It seems that when Gamine passed away and Imani took on her role as the nurturer of the family, she put her emotions on hold. She hasn't been the same since. She puts up a good front, but I know better. What she needs is a man in her life instead of only focusing on her career."

"Well, honey…" Her husband's voice trailed off as she continued to talk.

"You and I both know there's a reason why she really wants that estate, David. Gamine told her to invest in that estate, and Imani tries her best to fulfill all the dreams Gamine had for her. You know how much Imani hates to fail, and this man she's working with may not let her get the estate. Even Cyd and the girls avoid her at times now. They say she's at work twenty-four-seven, and if the girls can't get through to Imani, I don't know who can. Both my girls have issues with men. They need to find somebody and not focus solely on the company."

David draped a comforting arm over her shoulders and pulled her into his embrace. "Your compassion for others is one of the many reasons why I fell in love with you. But you have to realize that Imani needs to find her own way. And in due time, she will. Both of our daughters will. We have to be patient. Don't you agree?"

Hope listened to her husband. He always knew what to say to calm her down.

"You're right, honey…you're right."

"Well, let me show you just how right I am."

With a smile, he placed a passionate kiss on his wife's lips in hope of easing her worries.

## Chapter 7

Imani's hour-long soak in the tub had been much needed. After her bath, she put on her black satin nightgown and caught up on a little reading. Sitting on the balcony of her hotel room with a warm cup of chamomile tea, she listened to smooth R&B music playing in the background.

The night was so warm that it reminded her of a hot, summer night when she and the girls had taken an impromptu trip to Barbados. Ever since the company took off, they hadn't taken many impromptu vacations. Well, Cyd took trips like that, but they hadn't taken a trip together in a while. When she got back to Chicago, she'd be sure to mention that to the girls.

They all desperately needed a vacation. She decided she would use any downtime she had in Atlanta to relax and go shopping.

The evening breeze caught hold of her nightgown,

causing her to shiver. She had requested to be on a floor with few guests, and a quick glance around the outside perimeter of the hotel seemed to confirm that the hotel had honored that request.

Imani knew she shouldn't be wearing so little clothing on her balcony, but clothes had always been a bother to her, anyway. She preferred to feel comfortable and free. And she loved looking at the lit city skyscrapers.

Her thoughts drifted to Gamine. She quickly ran into her room and got a feather out of her stash—her personal way of connecting with Gamine. Closing her eyes, she said a silent prayer to Gamine, letting the feather catch in the wind and drift into the night sky.

When Imani opened her eyes, she saw a light turn on in the room next to hers. When the receptionist at the front desk had asked her if she would mind adjoining rooms, she figured it was okay since she was assured no one else was occupying the room. Imani wished she'd made the receptionist guarantee that the room would remain unoccupied throughout her stay because clearly, someone was there now. Since Imani wasn't decently dressed, she slowly made her way back into her room. She was just about to slide into bed when there was a knock on her door.

Slipping on her robe, she gasped as she looked through the peephole.

"It can't be," Imani said aloud.

She rubbed her eyes to see if she was imagining the person on the other side of the door. *Only one way to find out...*

She exhaled deeply and slowly opened the door.

"Hello, Imani," Daman said in a deep, husky voice. No one ever said her name like he did.

"Hello, Daman," Imani stated, her voice full of displeasure. "What are you doing in Atlanta? And more important, how did you know where I was staying or what room I was in?"

"You left that information with Vicky Gordon, the head of the volunteers. She informed me that she set up these arrangements for you and was more than happy to tell me where you were staying. I managed to book myself the connecting room."

The smoldering look Daman was giving her wasn't helping to calm the rising heat overtaking her body. Vicky obviously wouldn't have known that she shouldn't give out Imani's room number to her co-gala planner, so she couldn't be upset.

He was leaning on the outside of her door, smiling at her, knowing that she was annoyed he'd so casually stopped by.

"How long are you staying?" she asked in a dry tone.

"Since it's the weekend, I'm staying for a few days."

"Oh." Imani wasn't keen on his being in Atlanta at all but figured he knew that much.

"Vicky mentioned that you two had a meeting set up tomorrow morning at the location of the gala, so I took the liberty of inviting myself along. Is that okay with you?"

Imani knew Daman was baiting her to express her annoyance, and she refused to give him the satisfaction. "That's fine," she said through clenched teeth.

"Great. I'll knock on your door at 8:00 tomorrow morning so we can head to the next meeting together.

Have a good night." And with a sly smile, Daman walked back to his room.

Imani slammed her door and went to lie down in the comfortable bed. She disliked anyone telling her what to do and she disliked it even more when she couldn't get a word in edgewise to protest.

"The nerve of that man!" she yelled out loud.

The next morning, Imani and Daman walked into the Georgia World Congress Center and were greeted by an older couple and a group of five young men and women.

Vicky Gordon introduced herself to Imani and Daman and then the older woman introduced them to the man beside her. "This is my husband, Pete. Welcome to Atlanta, Ms. Rayne and Mr. Barker."

Imani and Daman exchanged handshakes with the couple.

"I'm excited to be here, and please call me Imani."

"And you can call me Daman," Daman replied after Imani. "I'm happy to be here, as well."

"That's great to hear, Imani and Daman," Vicky responded. "I'm the lead event manager here at the Georgia World Congress Center and my husband manages the facilities department. I will introduce you to a few people who flew in from Black Enterprise later today. As you know, they are hosting the gala and are very interested in discussing plans with you all and the rest of the team."

Imani had met a lot of entrepreneurs at last year's annual conference and respected the organization a great deal.

"I would like you both to meet a few of our student

volunteers," Vicky said, motioning toward the younger adults.

Imani noticed that each of the volunteers wore a T-shirt from The University of Georgia.

"Imani, Daman, my name is Jared Booker, and I'm the president of the Black Student Union campus organization at The University of Georgia. This is our vice president, Stephanie Rogers, treasurer, Michael Adams, editor of our monthly magazine, Paul White, and event and marketing director, Joan Griffin. We have many other volunteers from our organization who will be here to help with the gala, as well."

Imani shook hands with the enthusiastic five, reflecting on her own drive she had in college to make a difference. "It's very nice to meet you all. It means a lot to have student volunteers willing to dedicate their time."

Daman seemed equally impressed with the students. "We're glad your organization has offered to help with the gala. I look forward to working with you all."

"Now that introductions are out of the way, we can give you two a tour of the center," Vicky said to the group. "We'll start with the Thomas Murphy Ballroom, where the gala will take place."

When Imani had first walked into the Georgia World Congress Center, she'd admired the design, but thought it looked like many other conference centers. As Vicky led them deeper into the center, Imani was blown away by the breathtaking beauty of the ballroom.

The architectural design of the high ceiling was distinctively modern and the theater-style room had geometric carpeting with warm, brilliant tones. Unique sculptural designs were symmetrically stationed throughout the entire room. The overall effect was stunning.

The tour continued throughout the center, each room offering the same gorgeous decor; however, the Georgia Ballroom, where the pre-and-post-cocktail parties were to be held was Imani's favorite. It was also the room that received Daman's utmost approval.

"Vicky, this room is exquisite!" Daman exclaimed in complete awe.

Imani watched as he carefully viewed all the minor details of the room's decor. His strides were slow and precise and the concentration in his eyes was mesmerizing to her. She was so intensely consumed in watching Daman that she failed to notice the observant glance she was receiving from Vicky.

"I'm interested to know the history of this place," Daman said out loud to no one in particular. "The decor is modern so it must have been remodeled recently."

Vicky gleamed. "My husband would be able to answer all of your questions," Vicky said motioning toward the man beside her. "As facilities manager, he knows everything about this place."

"Pete," Daman said, gently slapping the older man on the shoulder. "Just the man I want to talk to. Can you tell me more about this place?"

"Sure," Pete said with a laugh. "The design truly is unique."

As the students followed Pete and Daman through the room, Vicky lingered behind with Imani.

"So how long have you and Daman worked together?" Vicky asked.

"This will be our first time working together. We haven't known each other long."

Vicky cocked her head to the side, clearly observing Imani.

"You're both well-rounded individuals. I was very impressed with each of you after reading the documents the Simses sent me. Are either of you married?"

"No, we're both single, and thanks for the compliment. Like I said, I haven't known Daman that long, but from what I know so far, he seems like he'll be a good business partner. You have nothing to worry about. We'll do a great job with the gala."

"Oh, I'm not worried at all. It just seems strange to me that a man and woman as accomplished as Daman and you haven't found the right person."

"He's not really my type, so I doubt you have to worry about a relationship between us interfering with our work."

"Oh, honey, I know you're a professional woman. Besides," Vicky said with an amused glint in her eyes, "I didn't say I was referring to Daman."

Imani's cheeks slightly flushed with embarrassment. She'd rather be doing anything else than having this conversation. It was her first time seeing Daman in his element, and she liked what she saw. She hoped Vicky didn't notice how enthralled she was with Daman, but people drew their own conclusions all the time, so she couldn't be concerned with what Vicky thought. Imani decided she needed to take the focus off herself.

"How long have you and Pete been married?"

"It will be forty-eight years this November. Although it feels like just yesterday I married that man. I was only eighteen and he nineteen when we decided to get married. Everyone told us we were too young, but we knew what we wanted. Four children and ten grandchildren later, that man is still as handsome and kindhearted as he was the first day we met."

Imani smiled at the love and devotion evident in her words. "My parents have a love like that. So did my grandparents. Actually, most of the couples in my family do, which is probably why I love talking with happily married couples. When I was younger, my cousins and friends would tease me that I would be the first one out of the group to get married. I always wanted a big wedding, three children and a relationship with my husband that was filled with the same kind of love my parents had."

"You're still young and have plenty of time to find the right man to settle down with."

Imani used to feel like a loving marriage was in her future, but over the past few years, her life had been an emotional roller coaster. Building a lasting relationship with someone was the last thing on her mind.

"I once thought that I would find the kind of love that inspired authors to write books but I don't think a love like that is in my future anymore."

"Well, my dear, you may be saying love isn't in your future, but your eyes seem to crave a special love that will last forever. No one knows what their future holds, Imani."

She understood what Vicky was trying to imply. "You sound like my mother."

Vicky winked. "Must be a smart woman."

Just as their conversation was ending, the rest of the group joined them.

"Let's continue with the tour," Vicky said to the group. "Then we can sit down and go over what needs to be done first. Much of the planning is already in the works."

As the tour continued, Vicky's words lingered in the air. Imani knew that Vicky was right. She didn't know what her future held. What she did know was that she gave up on her romantic, girlish wishes years ago when she decided to devote her time to her family and her company. Those were her two main loves and all she really needed in life. Not an even trade-off, but she was satisfied…or so she kept telling herself.

## Chapter 8

Later that evening, Daman and Imani were still at the Georgia World Congress Center, working hard on plans for the gala. They'd met with members of Black Enterprise that afternoon and were anxious to get down to business.

Although there were plenty of volunteers bustling around the office in the center, Daman was aware of every move Imani made. She was wearing a cream dress that was extremely flattering on her figure and her hair was in an updo, which showed off her high cheekbones and flawless makeup. He couldn't hide his appreciation for her style and was pretty sure others had noticed, as well.

It was almost 8:00 p.m. and the volunteers were finally wrapping up the day.

"I'm going to walk out the volunteers," Vicky said to Daman and Imani. "Then I have some last-minute paperwork to finish in my office. Are you both ready to leave?"

Daman was ready to leave, but Imani appeared to be in the middle of a project. "Daman, would you mind if we stay for fifteen more minutes?" Imani asked.

"No, I don't mind," Daman said as he took his laptop out of his bag and sat down at a nearby desk.

After Vicky and the volunteers left, Daman was alone with Imani. She floated around the room with an armful of papers, reviewing large to-do charts that hung on the walls and occasionally cross-referencing the information with the papers in her stack. Daman noticed her rub the back of her neck several times as if she were trying to get out a knot. He was pretending to do research, but in reality, Imani interested him more than doing any planning at the moment.

Imani stopped at the desk right across from Daman and plopped down her stack of papers. "I think I underestimated how tired I am," she said as she rested her head on the desk. "When Vicky returns, I'll be ready to leave."

Imani lifted her head and rolled her neck in a circular motion as she placed her hand on the back of her neck once more.

"Would you like me to massage that knot out of your neck?" Daman asked as he placed his laptop back in his bag.

Imani hadn't responded and continued rubbing her neck. When her eyes finally connected with his, her slight nod gave him the confirmation he was waiting for. When Daman reached Imani, he pulled her chair away from the desk so he could have better access to her neck.

When his hands initially touched her, she tensed under his grip. After a couple minutes of kneading the knot, Imani loosened up and relaxed. Her skin was as smooth as velvet and the soft moans escaping her lips sounded heavenly to his ears. He wished he was making her moan for another reason, but he'd take what he could get.

"Right there, Daman, don't stop," Imani whispered. Daman shifted his weight and wondered if she was purposely saying things that would remind him of sex. Her voice was sensual and the deeper he kneaded the knot, the more she leaned into him.

He wondered if she would make him stop if she realized he could see her lace bra peeking out of her dress. The dress wasn't low cut, but as he towered over her while massaging her neck, he couldn't help but look.

Daman's hands left her neck and ventured to her shoulders, performing a massage method that he usually saved for the bedroom. He'd been told by women that his hands were lethal, so naturally he began using this information to his advantage. He wondered how far Imani would let him go.

"Thank you," Imani said, breaking the direction of his thoughts. "I really appreciate it." She pushed the chair even farther from the desk so she could stand.

"My pleasure," Daman replied as he held out his hand to assist her. Taking his hand, Imani pushed from the seat and lost her footing. Daman caught her by the elbow and pulled her into his embrace.

He expected Imani to break from his grasp after

she regained her balance. After several seconds, she remained in his arms…their faces mere inches from each other. His eyes ventured to her glossy, pink lips. He never noticed how great lip gloss looked on a woman before. Although he liked how it looked, he wanted to kiss her lips until there was no shine left. There was nothing sexier than a thoroughly kissed woman, and he could imagine Imani's lips looked even better after being kissed.

Her felt her breath quicken as her eyes darted from his eyes to his mouth, as if mirroring his own thoughts. He wanted to kiss her, nibble on her lips. All he needed was one taste to feed his curiosity. He slowly eased her onto the desk so she could maintain her balance. He kissed her neck, softly at first and then with a little tongue. She moaned in pleasure, grasping his head to keep him in place. But he didn't want to kiss only her neck. He wanted more.

Tilting his head, he eased his lips closer to hers and was rewarded by her tilting her head in the opposite direction to accommodate his request.

Just as he was closing in on the lips he'd been thinking about all day, he heard footsteps coming down the hallway. Daman wasn't ready for Vicky to return, and he didn't want to let Imani up from the desk. But the mood was over. Her eyes said as much.

Pushing from the desk, he stood and helped her stand, as well.

"That didn't take long, did it?" Vicky asked as she walked into the office.

"No," Daman said rather quickly. Imani just nodded her head in agreement.

Vicky stopped in her tracks and looked back and forth from Daman to Imani, understandably curious about the difference in their demeanors.

"Are you two okay?" Vicky asked.

"We're fine," Imani answered as she went back to gather her belongings.

"Mmm, hmm. I wasn't born yesterday, you know," Vicky said, pointing her finger and eyeing them both. "But I'm good at pretending so I'll act like I didn't walk in on anything."

Imani smiled at Vicky's comment as she picked up her things. Daman followed suit, choosing not to say anything, either.

The drive back to the hotel was quiet. Imani knew they were each caught up in their thoughts about the kiss they almost shared. As Daman accompanied her to her hotel room door, she fumbled with the key card. Positioning himself directly behind her, he placed his hand over hers to help guide the card slowly into the slot. The act was incredibly erotic.

"Thank you," she said as she opened her door.

"You're welcome."

As they stared deeply into each other's eyes, Imani decided she had to make a move before he did. When they had been planning the gala, it was so easy being around him that she almost forgot she was on a mission to get the estate. But men like Daman always wanted to control the situation, and she needed to gain some ground.

"Would you like me to come in?"

"Yes."

Imani walked into the room, kicking off her heels while taking the pins out of her hair. As she leaned down to open the bottom dresser drawer, she stopped. She'd thought Daman would make himself comfortable on the sofa. Instead, he was standing a couple feet away from her, his eyes watching her every move. He was giving her that half smirk again—the one she found so sexy—and the temperature in the room rose fifty degrees.

"What are you thinking?"

He looked her up and down, and she wondered if he was ever going to answer. Then he zoned in on her feet. "This is my first time seeing your bare feet."

Imani glanced down at her feet, not understanding why that mattered. "Okay, what's your point?"

"Well, your feet are perfectly pedicured. They look very…suckable."

He licked his lips as he spoke, and she felt her breath leave her chest.

"I never took you for a foot man."

"There's a lot you still don't know about me. But we can fix that."

His statement caused her to blush, and she couldn't think of a comeback soon enough. He must have sensed her discomfort, and to her relief, he changed the subject.

"I admire your dedication and drive. You can tell that the student volunteers really admire all the advice you were giving them on planning events."

"Thanks. I admire your work ethic, too. I know you've planned events before, but considering it's not your main source of business, I was very impressed with how much you know."

For a brief moment, neither said anything. Imani was assessing Daman and she was pretty sure he was doing the same to her.

"Well, Miss Prim and Proper, I guess that means we have more in common than you thought. Imagine that."

His tone was cocky, and her face went from genuine to defensive in a matter of seconds.

"I never thought that we didn't have anything in common, but we do have different points of view on certain issues. You like to do things in your own time, and I like to get things done that need to get done. Our philosophies on life are different. Having a few similarities is to be expected. However, that doesn't discount the number of differences we obviously have."

Imani hated how he loved to rattle her nerves, and how easy she was making it for him to do that.

"We have plenty of similarities. But you put up a front with people you don't know. With me, what you see is what you get."

She crinkled her nose at him.

"Baby girl, the more you do that, the more turned on I get."

"I'm not your baby or your girl. And another thing, you use your bluntness to hide who you really are. You claim to be direct, yet you only say what you think people want to hear, not how you really feel. There's a distinct difference."

He looked a little taken aback with her statement, which let her know she was close to the truth.

"So you think you have me all figured out?"

She thought about his sarcastic question. She didn't think she had him all figured out, but she'd never admit that to him. When dealing with women, a man like Daman always had an agenda and in this case, he was baiting her.

"Yes, I do. You aren't as complicated as you'd like to think you are. There are many little things that I'm beginning to understand about your character, and sometimes your nonchalant attitude is misplaced."

She watched the amused expression leave his face and return in the same second.

"So let me get this straight. You're beginning to notice many little things about me. Your words, correct?"

"Yes. Your point?"

"Well, my point is that usually when a woman notices little things about a man, it's because she's interested in him. And every time I hint at you and I getting better acquainted, you make a face or frown."

"That's because you're irritating. When something irritates me, I can't help but notice it, or in this case, notice you, every time some annoying comment comes out of your mouth."

"So you don't deny being interested in me? Someone as arrogant and self-centered as myself?"

She didn't like where this conversation was headed. He worked her last nerve, and she couldn't understand why she even let him get to her. Truth be told, she did like him. Any woman would be crazy not to notice how sexy he was, and she knew he found her attractive. She even liked their bickering at times, but Daman always wanted to be the winner, and Imani was never the type to lose easily. She thought he had learned that two could play this game, but apparently he needed a reminder—a reminder he wouldn't forget.

"Honestly, I was attracted to you the first day we met. You were sitting in that conference room looking every bit of sexy in that suit. When our eyes locked, I felt it instantly. You know, that strain of unreleased passion…that seductive pull…that pure animal lust…" she said in a soft purr.

She could see he was trying hard to keep a straight face as she spoke. She felt the tension in his body even though she hadn't touched him yet. She was slowly backing him into a corner of the hotel room, staring deep into his eyes as she did so. She'd always been told that she should never play poker because all of her emotions were written in her eyes. This time, she'd use it to her advantage. She decided to think about everything wet dreams were made of, which was easy considering Daman was her target. She knew that he realized it was a game because with them, it had been that way since the beginning. Yet she continued to draw him into her web, and when he hit the corner table, she knew his cards were up. Now all he could do was play by *her* rules.

"Every time we are within ten feet of each other, I can't help but imagine your lips kissing, licking and sucking on every inch of me, and in return, you letting me have my way with you to do any and everything I please. I don't know what it is about you that makes me lose my damn mind with lust, but I can't resist the craving to have you buried deep, *deep* inside of me any longer."

Imani was playing with fire, but she didn't care. Seduction was all part of the game they had started, and she planned on finishing this round on top. Literally.

By now, Daman was sitting on the table for support. Imani slowly hiked up her dress, revealing her shapely thighs, as she straddled him on the table. She loved how utterly defenseless he was now that she had taken charge. If she hadn't been attracted to him, this side of her would have never come out. Imani hoped her next move would leave him speechless. She had to break his self-assurance.

She inched closer and closer to his face. She slowly kissed his neck, then traced the outline of his ear with her tongue, making sure her touch was light and soft. She pulled his earlobe into her mouth and softly rolled the lobe with her tongue. She was rewarded by a shudder from Daman and repeated the same sweet torture to his other side. Taking a moment to catch her breath, she glanced at his lips. They looked ripe for the picking.

The moment her lips touched his, she knew her suspicions were correct. He really did have a sexual hold on her that no man ever had before. Daman quickly took control of the kiss and slowly began to probe her lips apart. His tongue darted in and out like it was making love to her mouth. She met him stroke for stroke and ground herself on his manhood.

Daman's hands roamed everywhere as her hips increased in tempo. A soft moan escaped her lips, and Daman's hands moved to grip her thighs so she wouldn't fall off the table. Their tongues were playing a game of hide and seek, neither staying hidden for long. With each stroke of his tongue, she matched his movements, the butterflies in her stomach growing stronger than ever. Finally, his hands made their way to her behind.

When she heard him moan in satisfaction, she knew she had to stop the kiss before it went any further.

Looking into his eyes, she couldn't believe a simple game had turned into one of the most passionate first kisses of her life. She could tell that neither one of them could really process how overwhelming that kiss was, which had her wondering: *who was seducing whom?*

She slid off Daman's lap and attempted to compose herself. No such luck. Her dress was twisted, she knew her hair was a mess and her face felt flushed.

Clearing his throat, Daman stood and adjusted his pants. She tried to will her eyes to look away from his aroused state, but she couldn't. He was trying to hide it, but she wanted to tell him not to bother. She'd felt the effect she had on him, and she was sure neither of them would forget how good it felt anytime soon.

"It's been a pleasure, but I think I should be heading out."

Although his desire to depart was sudden, she was ultimately relieved because they both needed time to think about that kiss. Neither of them was in the right state of mind to deal with it at that moment.

"Let me walk you out."

Daman hesitated when he reached the door, and Imani wondered if he would decide to turn the tables on her.

Instead, he bent down to kiss her forehead and walked out the door.

# Chapter 9

Imani arrived at the home of Z105 thirty minutes before she was due to go on air. Before she walked into the building, she smoothed out her black pencil skirt and checked the first buttons of her silk blouse, satisfied that she wasn't showing too much cleavage. Once inside, she gave her name to the receptionist, who called to inform the production team that she had arrived.

Imani was excited to be on *The Jimmy King Morning Show* and had been an avid listener for years. Elite Events had been lucky enough to throw a private birthday party for Jennifer Hudson after the company she originally hired failed to be responsive to her ideas. When Jimmy King expressed his appreciation for her work, she jumped at the opportunity to sarcastically suggest he have her on his show.

As the production assistant led her down the hallway, she heard Jimmy King tell the listeners they would go on a commercial break and return with a member of Elite Events Incorporated. Seconds later, she was being escorted into the recording room.

"Hello, Jimmy. It's very nice to see you again," Imani stated as she extended her hand.

"Nice to see you, too, Imani." Jimmy returned her handshake and continued with introductions. "This is Tammy and right next to her is Monique."

"Nice to meet you both," Imani replied as she returned their handshakes.

"Uh, aren't you forgetting somebody?" Tommy said in a high-pitched, yet deep voice.

"Oh, yeah, and on the end there is my best friend Tommy," Jimmy added.

Imani laughed as she shook Tommy's hand, thinking that the two were as funny in person as they were on the air.

"Nice to meet you, too, Tommy."

"Likewise," Tommy said.

Imani was prepped and ready for her interview in no time.

"All right, welcome back everybody. Here with us today is Ms. Imani Rayne from Elite Events Incorporated here in Chicago. If y'all don't know them, you better ask somebody. Welcome to the show, Imani."

"Thanks for having me, Jimmy. I'm very happy to be here."

"Folks, I attended a very extravagant birthday party for Jennifer Hudson a couple months ago, and I was blown away by what these women did. Imani, why don't you tell the listeners a little bit about yourself and your company."

"Sure. Mya Winters, Cydney Rayne, Lexus Turner and I founded Elite Events Incorporated six years ago. Our event-planning business is among the top in the country and has earned us a recurring appearance in *Forbes Magazine*. Besides planning elaborate and elite events, we also publish a bimonthly magazine and own several Boys & Girls Clubs across the Midwest. There is a strong need for Elite Events in this society, and my partners and I will continue growing our business by taking our company to new heights."

"Hey, now," Tammy chimed in with excitement. "What you ladies are doing at Elite Events Incorporated is inspirational."

"Thank you, Tammy. We couldn't have been successful without each other, our families and friends and all of our supporters who believed in us."

"True for us all," Jimmy said. "What other types of parties do you plan?"

"We plan everything," Imani responded. "Corporate events, birthdays, weddings, festivals, concerts, album-release parties, movie-release parties…you name it, we can plan it. We've even planned a family reunion."

"Ah, naw," Jimmy said. "You mean to tell me that there was a family out there who paid you to contact all their family to plan a reunion?"

"Yes," Imani said with a laugh. "Actually, we've planned several."

"Well, folks, I've heard it all. Paying somebody to deal with your family because you don't want to. Imani, we wish you the best in your continued success with Elite Events Incorporated. Okay, now I would like to talk about your role in the First Annual Performance and Achievement Awards Gala this year."

Soft music began playing indicating that they needed to take a break.

"On second thought, wait until after the break to give the listeners details on that event. Ladies and gentlemen, when we come back, we're going to hear more from Imani, and we have another special guest here with us today."

They were all still laughing at Jimmy's last comment about family reunions as they went off air.

"Looks like our other guest is here," Tommy said, interrupting the laughter and leaving the recording room. As Imani turned toward the glass window to see who Tommy was greeting, her laugh stopped short. His back was to her, but she had no doubt in her mind whom that back belonged to.

"Oh, goodness," Imani whispered to herself. Apparently, she didn't whisper low enough because she got the attention of Tammy and Monique.

"Hmm, who is that?" Monique asked.

"That's Daman Barker," Tammy answered. "I guess Tommy told Jimmy we should have him on the show."

"We're both planning the gala," Imani added. "I didn't know he was going to be on the show. Does he personally know Tommy?"

"Tommy said they met during his days of stand-up comedy," Tammy responded.

Imani was trying to remain calm, although she was far from it. She could *not* believe his nerve. Daman knew she would be on the show and deliberately chose not to tell her that he would be there, too. Even worse, she bet he wasn't even interested until she'd mentioned something.

"What am I missing out on over there?" Jimmy said loudly. Daman turned at the sound of Jimmy's voice and his eyes locked to Imani's. As Tommy and Daman walked back inside the recording room, Imani wished she could wipe that smug look off his face.

Tommy introduced him to the others before coming to her. One look at Tommy and she could tell she'd been set up. He was grinning way too hard.

"Hello, Imani," Daman said in a husky voice.

"Hello," Imani responded, trying to sound as casual as possible. "Fancy meeting you here."

"Tommy and I go way back," Daman said, grasping Tommy by the shoulder. "I told him the show would be so much better if both the planners of the gala were present."

Imani highly doubted that's how their conversation went but chose not to say anything. The crew quickly prepped Daman for on air and just her luck, they sat him next to her.

"Okay, folks, we're back, and I'm with Imani Rayne and our new guest, co-planner of the Black Enterprise First Annual Performance and Achievement Awards Gala, Mr. Daman Barker. Daman, we're glad to have you on the show."

"Thanks for having me, Jimmy."

"Now, before the break, Imani was going to tell us about the gala, but either of you feel free to answer. Let's start with telling the people what exactly is the gala."

Imani took the first question. "Black Enterprise has

thrown over fifteen entrepreneur conferences and expos that allowed business owners the opportunity to network with other business owners and learn the keys to owning a successful business. This year, they are throwing their First Annual Performance and Achievement Awards Gala that will be the premier destination event for business owners and entrepreneurs. The companies being honored at this event are companies that have demonstrated success in all areas and resulted in proven success in their business."

"I've personally attended quite a few of their conferences and they are definitely something all business owners and entrepreneurs must go to," Jimmy said. "Now, will this event be open to the public?"

Imani nodded for Daman to answer this question. "The gala is by invite only, however, all of our pre-events are open to the public."

As Daman continued to explain the different workshops going on, Imani was still trying to figure out what she would do to get him back. She hated being tricked and even more, she hated surprises. Daman had been doing both ever since they met. She was so wrapped in her thoughts, she realized she'd missed a little more of the conversation than she'd planned.

"I've planned a lot of successful business events, but I have two full-time day jobs."

*Two? What is the second one?*

"I'm vice president of Barker Architecture, and I'm the newest partner of R&W Marketing."

Imani's eyes grew wide in surprise. He couldn't be talking about the company that her neighborhood friends, Taheim and Jaleen owned.

"That's right," Tammy said. "I remember seeing an article about the partnership last month."

Imani couldn't believe how out of touch she was. Not only was she an extremely detailed person but also very good at noticing a curveball before it was thrown. Apparently, she was losing her touch.

She noticed Jimmy and Tammy observing her closely and attempted to take her eyes off Daman. But the more he talked, the more she became fascinated with how little she knew about him.

"Oh, okay," Jimmy chimed in, interrupting Daman. "I see what all that chatter was about before we went on air. Y'all got a thang going on between you, right?" Jimmy motioned his hands between Daman and Imani.

"Absolutely not," Imani answered with an edge to her voice. Daman laughed off the comment, which irritated her even more.

"Oh, yeah, I know I'm right. What do you think, Tammy?"

"Hmmm, I hate to say it Imani, but I agree with Jimmy. I can feel the chemistry between you and Daman."

Great. Now everyone thought they had a *thing* going on.

"Daman, my man," Tommy said. "Y'all got something going on?"

"What Imani and I have is our business," Daman said with a laugh. "Besides, men never kiss and tell."

Imani gave Daman a swift punch in the arm. She couldn't believe the audacity of him and the fact that the radio cast was laughing so hard was making the situation that much worse.

"Listeners, if looks could kill, Daman would be dead right now."

Imani sunk a little more in her seat, thinking about how many of her friends and family members were listening to the show. Daman must have sensed her discomfort and took pity on her because he tried to clean up the situation.

"Imani is a beautiful, talented and educated woman. However, we aren't dating. Secret or otherwise."

"Okay, playa," Jimmy said, dismissing Daman's comment.

"Well, Imani and Daman, it's been great having you on the show, and I must say that I definitely didn't think we'd be making love connections today, but hey, on *The Jimmy King Morning Show* anything's possible. I wish you both the best of luck with your businesses and your budding romance."

"Jimmy! Leave them alone," Tammy reprimanded right before the break music went on.

Imani and Daman both thanked Jimmy and the cast before leaving the recording room. When they were on the other side of the glass window, Imani grabbed Daman by the arm and led him to a corner by the door.

"You work with Taheim and Jaleen?"

Now it was Daman's turn to look surprised. She assumed he was taken aback because she stated the names as if she knew them personally.

"Yes, they're my partners," he answered, leaning against the wall. "We announced our partnership last month. How do you know them?"

"Our families have been friends for decades. I grew

up with both of them, but I haven't seen them in a while. I've been very busy, too busy— clearly."

She recalled the invitation she'd declined when her partners went out with Taheim and Jaleen for drinks. "Did you know about me before we met with Mr. and Mrs. Sims?"

"No, I didn't know you. Your name was brought up during a meeting with Taheim and Jaleen days after we met, but they never mentioned knowing you personally."

Imani looked into his eyes and could tell he was telling the truth. Apparently, they had both been misled. She was going to kill her friends for not telling her that Daman was partners with Taheim and Jaleen. As much as they kept in contact with Taheim and Jaleen, there was no way they hadn't known.

She was trying her best to remain angry at Daman for secretly bombarding her on-air time. Yet, all she could think about was how Daman's scent was doing crazy things to her body. Being close to him was never a good thing since she had to concentrate extremely hard to try to keep her body temperature leveled.

"Don't look at me like that," Daman said to Imani. "Or I'm liable to kiss you again."

"Not here," Imani replied. "I mean, not ever."

"Not ever, really?"

The lower part of her body knew she was lying. "We'll see," she said, feeling a little bolder than usual.

Jimmy's voice filled the room, disrupting the moment. "If y'all two are finished wooing one another, I'd like to get on with my show." Imani glanced around trying to figure out how he could hear their conversation when he was in the recording room. More important, how could she hear him so clearly?

"Daman, would you please flip that switch that you're leaning on so we won't hear you and Imani in the background," Jimmy said with a laugh. "Listeners, if you could see the way these two are looking into each other's eyes, mark my words, we're making love connections on *The Jimmy King Morning Show* today."

Daman flipped the switch, but it was a little too late. Imani couldn't recall ever being this embarrassed. She was a private person and being teased on a popular radio show about issues she hadn't even faced yet, was not her idea of fun.

"I need to leave," Imani said as she rushed from the room.

## Chapter 10

On the drive back to his hotel, Daman wondered if he should go to Imani's condo and check on her. She'd left the show abruptly, so he didn't get a chance to say anything after they noticed their private conversation wasn't so private after all. Looking back, he wasn't sure that it had been a good idea to refrain from telling her he would be on the show. After it ended, she'd barely made eye contact with him. Daman had gotten a chance to talk to Tommy briefly before he left Z105. He could still hear Tommy's insightful words—"Word of advice, if you want her, you better move fast. Trust me."

At the time, Daman was too focused on Imani rushing out of the building to give his words a second thought. But Tommy had a point. He knew a lot of good men were looking for a good woman. Hell, she'd instantly impressed him the first time they met.

Somehow, he ended up in front of her condo. He

couldn't help but wonder if she would tell the doorman to let him up, just to slam the door in his face. At least if she let him up, he would be able to steal a glance at the face that grew sexier every time she turned her anger toward him. He told the doorman he was there to see Imani and shockingly, she told him to let Daman up.

"Uh...hi."

He noticed her hesitation before she fully opened the door. "Hi. Come on in."

After she closed the door, Daman walked into the room and examined Imani's face. He couldn't tell what she was thinking.

"I'd like to apologize for not telling you I would be on the show beforehand. The last thing I wanted to do was imply that we were in a relationship."

Imani tilted her head to the side and sighed before responding. "I know, and I really don't feel like arguing with you after the evening I just had."

He watched her face soften.

"Did you tell Taheim and Jaleen you would be on the show?"

"Yes."

"And they didn't say anything?"

Daman shook his head, finally seeing a couple more pieces of the puzzle fit together. "Nope. Now that I think about it, Taheim spilled his coffee when I mentioned your name a couple of weeks ago and was completely normal every time I mentioned your name after that. They told me they'd heard of you and your partners, but they didn't say they knew y'all personally."

"I'm not surprised. My friends are sneaky, and Taheim and Jaleen love getting one past me. There's no doubt in my mind that they knew we shared that con-nection."

He knew how she meant the comment, but that didn't stop his body from reacting to the way she said *connec-tion*. He'd like to connect with her in a couple differ-ent ways, none of which included their friends. "I see."

For the first time that night, Daman noticed what she was wearing. She'd traded her business attire for a blue negligee that only hit midthigh and was clinging softly to her body. She hadn't bothered to put on a robe. He wondered what she had on underneath and fought the urge to pull her into a smoldering kiss.

As his eyes raked further over her face and body, he was mesmerized by the way her tongue dipped in and out of her mouth when she spoke. When he glanced back into her eyes, he felt the heat. That was all the encouragement he needed.

He pulled her closer and gently circled her lips with his tongue. At first, she wasn't responding. Then sud-denly, she began to suckle his lips, starting at the cor-ners and unrelentingly journeying around his entire mouth. When she softly kissed the last untouched por-tion of his mouth, the need became too strong for him. He probed her mouth open with his tongue.

"Mmmm, you taste like sweet honey. I missed this taste." His tongue left her mouth and made its way to her neck. "Smells like vanilla jasmine...intoxicat-ingly erotic."

Daman quickly decided one taste wouldn't be enough. He craved to be buried inside of her, but the game had changed now. He knew she was different the minute he laid eyes on her. Knowing that she knew his friends made it even worse. In the past, he never cared if he shamelessly slept with women and then acted indifferent to them after the moment of passion had passed. But Taheim and Jaleen were protective of the people they were close to and would definitely chew him out if he treated Imani like he did other women. He had to be straight with her.

"Imani, I have to be honest with you. I'm happy being a bachelor, and I don't have time in my life for a serious relationship. I get portrayed as a great catch, but I will never be the type you'd want to marry. I just can't imagine living my life any other way than I do now."

The blank look on her face was hard to read. She began to push him away, and instantly, he regretted ruining the moment.

Imani was a little taken aback by his bluntness but appreciated his honesty. There was a time when she wanted to get married and raise a family just like hers. She knew she was the marrying type, but she couldn't remember the last time she'd thought about those things. Being there for her family was her first priority and her career was her second. There was no room for anything else. Her life was hectic enough without the trouble that came with relationships, and right now, all she needed was to feed her hunger.

"Well, I guess that's great to hear because I'm not looking for a relationship, either. I think our attraction is pretty clear, and I can find many uses for a man like you."

He raised an eyebrow at her. "Uses like what?"

Imani fiddled with the buttons on his shirt as she tilted her head to the side and stared into his eyes. She was battling with her conscience, unsure of what to do next. She knew she wanted him sexually. She just didn't know how long she should hold out. Men like Daman only wanted one thing, and after they got it, they moved on to the next conquest. She could handle a "friends with benefits" relationship, *but* could she handle being in the spotlight for the next few months with the press in their personal business?

Giving him one last head-to-toe look, she made up her mind.

"Sexual uses, Daman. I could use a man like you to fulfill my sexual needs. That is, if you think you can handle me."

Daman smiled, showing off his pearly white teeth. "I can handle you any way you like. Soft…rough… nasty…I've been known to show women a good time. The real question is do you think you can handle what I have to give?"

Imani sighed. She hadn't had a lot of sexual partners in her life, but she'd had enough to know that it was all the same. She heard stories from women who boasted about sex like it was the greatest thing in the world, but she failed to see what all the fuss was about. She liked sex just as much as the next woman, but to her it was just another stress reliever. Looking at Daman, she knew he would be different, but she refused to give him the satisfaction of knowing that.

"Everything is a competition with you. Sex is sex. What could you possibly give me that I haven't already had?"

The determined look in Daman's eyes caused her breath to catch. Without words, he was telling her to prepare herself for a sexual eruption unlike any she'd ever experienced. The next few seconds were all a blur. One minute she was standing, and the next minute she was sprawled on the floor with Daman positioned over her.

"I hope you don't get upset with me when I say this, Imani, but as tense as you've been since I met you, I highly doubt that a man has thoroughly had sex with you recently, if ever. Otherwise, you'd know that even though sex is sex, the fun comes in all the ways you bring about that pleasure. All you need is the right partner."

While he was talking, he was kissing her neck and shoulders.

"It's about the chemistry being so strong that you don't even have to touch the person to feel that intense sexual pull."

He untied her negligee and gasped. Imani didn't know whether it was a good or bad gasp until he grinned, and his hands started roaming underneath the silky material.

"It's about admiring the beauty of one another's bodies and linking in an unexplainable yet pleasurable way."

She felt his head dip down and alternate licking her breasts. He gently sucked each nipple, and just when Imani thought he was finished, he started the process all over again. She was only vaguely aware of how exposed she was, but she did notice that he was still wearing all his clothes.

His tongue continued its downward exploration of her body, licking each crevice and dipping in and out her belly button. When he reached her thighs, she held her breath in anticipation. In previous relationships, the men she'd dated only teased one spot. She wondered if Daman would be the same way. He abruptly stopped and looked into her eyes.

"It's about feeding your desire and sexing that person to the point that they can't see straight. I've wanted to devour you since the first day we met, and now I get my chance."

The minute his mouth covered her center, she knew Daman was not like other men. He kissed her lightly at first, as if preparing her body for his mouth's attack. As his licks grew more aggressive, Imani couldn't do anything but grab the rug she was lying on.

His tongue found her pink nub, and he gently sucked the sensitive area. When she felt like she would explode with satisfaction, he would stop and dip his tongue inside her center. She began clinching her vaginal muscles as his tongue quickened its in-and-out rotation between her core and her clitoris.

Imani's lower body came off the floor as he lifted her hips so his tongue could go deeper.

"Oh…goodness. I can't take it…it's too much."

Apparently, Daman didn't care because he increased the pace of his tongue and squeezed her butt tighter so she couldn't go anywhere. Between her moans, she heard him speaking.

"Do you really want me to stop?"

She didn't know how she found the words, but she managed to give him a truthful answer. "No, don't stop. Whatever you do, don't stop."

"Good, because you taste too good for me to stop."

"Really?"

"Yeah, really. You taste just like candy."

"Ahhh…" Her moans grew more and more frantic.

"That's it. Let it out, baby."

Between his naughty words and the onslaught of his tongue, Imani was losing her mind. She didn't know how he managed to talk and please her at the same time. There she was, stuck in midair between Daman's mouth and his hands, and all she could do was hold on for dear life. She'd never experienced something so erotic. As her body broke into several convulsions, her moaning and screaming grew louder. She was so overcome with passion that she barely recognized Daman placing her back on the floor.

Instantly, her mind began racing with what would happen next. Everything had happened so fast. One minute they had been talking and the next she was moaning with gratification. She could barely think straight. No doubt he would want to have sex after that.

As if reading her thoughts, Daman answered her question. "Don't worry, we aren't having sex tonight." He stood and helped her off the floor. She thought he was leaning in to kiss her, but instead, he retied her negligee. Imani was unsteady and couldn't believe how weak her body felt. She couldn't recall ever having an orgasm that strong. She leaned into Daman for support, wondering if she should be embarrassed of the state she was in.

Daman gently kissed her lips. "Please don't be self-conscious. You have nothing to be ashamed about. Plus, I think I know how good I made you feel if your screams were any indication of that."

Imani nudged Daman in his side, causing him to let out a fake cry. There was hunger in his eyes, and she could feel the heat radiating between them. She looked down at his pants and saw his engorged sex.

"Why did you tell me not to worry about sex tonight?"

Daman smiled down at her and kissed her forehead. Slowly, he turned and began walking toward the door. When he reached for the knob, he looked back at her and shook his head. "You're one tempting woman, and trust me when I say I would love to take you right here. But now doesn't seem like the right time, and we both know that brain of yours hasn't finished processing what's going on between us yet." He gave her a kiss on her forehead. "Have a good night."

She was still standing in the same position minutes after the door had closed.

*That man is dangerous*. But she wanted him. That much was obvious. The businesswoman in her was on high alert, and she had to remember the reason they were thrown together in the first place. Unfortunately, none of those thoughts were running through her mind at the moment. The only thought on her mind right now was how he'd managed to get her naked while he remained fully clothed.

## Chapter 11

The rest of the week went by much smoother than Daman would have suspected. When he left Imani's condo on Monday, he'd stayed up half the night because he couldn't sleep. He knew he'd made the right decision by leaving, but it didn't stop him from visualizing what could have happened. He surprised himself by maintaining his self-control.

Sitting on his stationary jet at the Aurora Municipal Airport, he tried convincing himself that he was more excited that it was Friday and almost the weekend than he was about seeing Imani. After talking with Vicky, Daman and Imani had decided to visit Atlanta again on the weekend. Wth the gala so close, planning was crucial, and it was easier to organize the event in person rather than conference calls.

Through the window of the jet, he saw Imani step

out of a taxi. She had agreed to ride with him in his jet as opposed to taking a commercial flight.

"Hi, Imani. It's nice to see you again," Daman said as she approached the jet entrance.

"Hello, Daman." Imani gasped as they stepped inside.

"Is something wrong?"

"No, I'm just surprised. I didn't know your private jet would be so large. I assumed it would be smaller, like other private jets I've been in."

He laughed at the look of awe he saw in her eyes.

"As much as I would love to take full credit for this beauty, I can't. It belongs to the company. When Barker Architecture went from two offices to ten offices in four years, two being international offices, my dad invested in a dream he'd always had for Barker Architecture. A private jet. Now with fifteen offices and four being international, I can't imagine not having it."

"Well, it's gorgeous."

"I appreciate that. Feel free to make yourself comfortable. My staff can get you anything you need to drink."

Imani lifted her left eyebrow and crossed her arms over her chest. "Your staff?"

Daman grinned at her stance. He knew she wouldn't be standing like that if she knew the effect it was having on him, seeing her breasts pressed up against her shirt.

"By staff, I mean James. He worked with my father since before I could remember and insisted that he continue working for me. He's more like family."

James approached Imani and introduced himself before heading to the back of the jet.

Imani leaned into Daman so that James couldn't overhear what she was saying. "I hope you don't work him too hard."

James laughed loudly, getting Daman and Imani's attention.

"I'm fine, young lady. Daman puts up with this old goat, but I know he can find better. But don't let this eighty-one-year-old body fool you. I know how to keep up."

The surprised look on Imani's face made Daman laugh.

"I'm sure you can, James. You remind me a lot of my grandfather."

James stood a little taller. "Must be a dashing fellow."

Imani and Daman laughed. They took their seats just as the copilot was coming toward them with a worried look on his face.

"There seems to be a problem, Mr. Barker."

"What is it? Is everything okay?"

"Yes, but we were listening to the radio, and they said that there was a massive storm that just hit the States."

"Can we still make it to Georgia before nightfall?"

"Yes, sir. But the storm seems to have hit a small town in Florida. All communication between the town and neighboring cities has been lost. Sir, it's pretty close to where your mother lives."

Daman felt the air rush out of his lungs. If anything happened to his mother, he'd be devastated. "How bad was the storm?"

"From what I can gather, most of the buildings are

still standing. The winds were extremely powerful, and the citizens of Florida said they haven't seen a storm this bad in years."

Daman glanced at Imani before turning back to the pilot. "Change of plans. Get us as close to my mom's town as possible."

"Yes, sir."

James had made some calls and had a car waiting for them when the jet landed. He'd decided to wait with the jet in case someone needed to contact Daman.

Imani kept telling herself that Daman's mother would be okay, but as they got closer to the town, she began to have doubts.

"Oh, my goodness." She hadn't meant for the words to escape her mouth, but it was hard to believe that a storm was capable of causing so much damage. The downtown area had a few shops that seemed to be holding up better than others. Ambulances and fire trucks filled some areas, but it was heartbreaking to see people scattered throughout the streets, frantically looking for more help. They stopped the car several times to pass out water bottles that James had stocked in the trunk.

Daman tried calling his mother several times, but the phone wouldn't connect. "The cell towers must be down."

It was harder to see the damage as they neared the countryside, since everything was spread so far apart.

"A lot of houses are still standing in the distance."

Her voice was hopeful, but Daman only gave her a small smirk. He'd already lost one parent, and it was evident that his mom was his number-one priority since his father's death. It took them two hours to get to his mother's house, but it seemed that the town only had a little damage. Daman pulled the car up in front of a two-story house. Even in the nasty weather, Imani could tell the house was beautiful.

Daman hopped out the car so fast Imani hadn't even realized it had come to a complete stop.

"Mom…Mom…are you here!"

Imani took off after Daman, not caring that mud and debris from the storm were ruining her clothes. His mother swung open the front door at the same time Daman made it onto the porch.

"Daman! Oh, baby, I'm so happy to see you! One minute I was listening to the news and the next, the power was out. But police officers and firemen visited the houses to tell us that our town was not greatly affected and that there was no reason to evacuate. The worst is over."

They embraced in a big hug before Daman stepped back to examine his mother. "I'm so glad you're okay. Your town does look fine, but I was worried after what we saw driving down here in other towns."

"We, baby?"

Imani chose this time to step out from around the upturned lawn chair she'd been leaning against. Watching the exchange between Daman and his mother had been heartwarming.

"Hello, Mrs. Barker. My name is Imani Rayne. It's a pleasure to meet you."

Imani was reaching out to shake hands, but instead, Patricia pulled her into a tight hug. Imani hugged her back, assuming she was still flustered from the storm.

However, when she glanced into the woman's eyes, she noticed she was tearing up.

"Mrs. Barker, is everything okay?"

Mrs. Barker quickly wiped away the tears that had fallen before responding.

"I'm so happy I'm okay, that I'm overcome with emotion. I apologize for squeezing you so tightly, Imani, and might I add that Imani is a beautiful name."

She looked into the woman's face and felt a familiarity that she couldn't quite explain. They only met minutes ago, but something about her was comforting. She instantly felt at ease with Mrs. Barker.

"That's okay. I needed the hug, anyway."

Mrs. Barker placed her hand over her chest and laughed.

"How did you and Daman meet? Are you dating?"

Imani looked at Daman for him to answer. "No, Mom. We aren't dating. I told you about Imani over the phone. We're hosting the gala together."

"Oh, that's right. You never told me her name…or how beautiful she was. Imani, are you married? I don't see a ring."

Imani caught Daman rolling his eyes. It was clear that Mrs. Barker was anxious for her son to settle down.

"No, ma'am. I'm not married."

"Oh. Well, in that case, why don't the two of you come in, and I can whip us up something to eat."

As they walked into the house, Imani was amazed that everything was still in place.

"Daman, can you go and start the generator?"

"Sure, Mom," Daman said and minutes later, they had power.

"Thanks, baby," Mrs. Barker said when he returned.

Imani walked around the living room and admired the mahogany wood. There were four tables that all matched and were very similar to a set that she acquired after Gamine passed away. Knowing Daman's eyes were on her, she turned to smile at him.

"Your table set is beautiful, Mrs. Barker. My grandmother left me a similar set. I love mahogany wood."

"Thank you. I went to a lot of vintage stores to find them."

Daman glanced from the tables to Imani and snapped his fingers in recognition. "I knew your table set looked familiar. It reminded me of my mom's."

Imani giggled at his sudden burst of acknowledgment. Neither noticed that Mrs. Barker was intently watching their interaction.

"There's nothing going on between you two?"

Imani gulped hard and pretended to attentively study some art displayed on the wall. *Like mother, like son... straight to the point.*

"Mom, drop it."

"Don't *Mom* me. You two aren't fooling anybody. I can see it with my own eyes." She was relentless.

"You remind me a little of my grandmother. She always got straight to the point," Imani said. "Not that there is a point to be made in this situation."

Mrs. Barker grinned before her eyes grew sad. "I'm sorry to hear about your grandmother, Imani."

She looked at Mrs. Barker and wondered what Daman had told her about her Gamine's passing. Daman gave his mom a questionable look.

"Imani said that her grandmother left her a similar

table set, and I keep up with the news, son. I know who Imani is, and I know she's a Burrstone." She glanced at Imani. "And I must say that you are a very remarkable woman. I'm sure your family is very proud of you."

"Thank you, Mrs. Barker."

"You're welcome, sweetie. I hope you both are staying the night."

Daman stole a glance in Imani's direction. She pretended not to notice until she heard him speak.

"Imani, are you okay with that?" Daman asked.

She instantly felt two pairs of eyes on her.

"Well, Imani?" The question came from Mrs. Barker. Imani looked back and forth between the two before settling her eyes on Mrs. Barker.

"Sure, Mrs. Barker. I don't see any reason why we can't stay. I wish we could contact Vicky and let her know we won't arrive until tomorrow."

"Oh, don't worry about that," Daman explained. "I sent her a quick email before we landed just in case we didn't make it to Georgia tonight."

Imani nodded her head in acknowledgment. She tried to tear her gaze away from him, but he was a mystery she couldn't quite solve. He commanded her attention at the strangest times. They were strictly partners for the gala, nothing more, and she knew she would be better off if she reminded herself of that fact.

Mrs. Barker interrupted her thoughts.

"Well, since that's taken care of, I will quickly show you your rooms. After that, Imani and I will prepare something to eat."

They both followed Mrs. Barker upstairs. Imani willed her nerves to go away, but it didn't work. Ever since she'd met this man, it seemed like they couldn't go a day without their paths crossing.

"Here we are. Daman will be in this room, and Imani, you'll be in the other."

She gestured for each of them to check out their separate rooms. As Imani walked into her room, she noticed more antique wood. The bed set was gorgeous and looked like the vintage bed set her grandmother had left to Cyd. The similarity was uncanny, since she always thought the antiques her grandmother collected were one of a kind.

Suddenly, the air around her grew thick with awareness. She glanced toward the bathroom and saw Daman fill the entrance. She was so wrapped up in the beautiful antique furniture that she hadn't noticed the connecting bathroom. *Someone really doesn't want me to get a good night's sleep.*

"Oh, I hope you both don't mind the connecting rooms. These are the only guest rooms in the house." Sensing Imani's reservations, Mrs. Barker continued, "Imani, you're more than welcome to sleep in my room, instead."

She thought about the offer. She'd shared a connecting room with Daman at the hotel, so she saw no reason why they couldn't share a bathroom now. "No, thank you, Mrs. Barker. I'm fine with this arrangement."

Daman hadn't said a word for the last ten minutes. Even now, he just stood there staring at her.

"Oh, good," Mrs. Barker said as she happily clasped her hands together. "Imani, dear, come downstairs with me."

Daman glanced in his mother's direction as if he'd

been caught doing something he shouldn't have. Imani pretended not to notice the situation, but it was obvious that his mother saw how long his eyes had been glued to her. Imani appreciated the interruption and hurriedly followed Mrs. Barker.

They decided to prepare skirt steaks, green beans, macaroni and a salad. Imani's stomach was growling just thinking about eating everything. She and Mrs. Barker worked well together. She felt right at home with Daman's mom. They didn't do much talking while cooking, but the silence was comforting, and the occasional smile that passed between them felt natural.

"You know, my son seems quite taken by you, Imani. I've never seen him this way around a woman. I can tell you care for him, too."

The statement caught Imani off guard, and she struggled to maintain her composure. "Your son and I do work well together, but we haven't known each other long. I'm sure he seems taken by me because we've been together so much lately."

She could feel Mrs. Barker's eyes studying her while she tossed the salad.

"I may have only known you for a couple hours, but I know my son. I can tell when he's interested in a woman. Daman isn't easily impressed by the opposite sex, but you have definitely gotten his attention."

"You think so?" Imani hadn't meant for her voice to raise and sound expectant. She tried to clear up the mishap. "I meant that we both have the same view on relationships. That is, we don't want one, need one, or have time for one. I must admit that I'm impressed with Daman, too, and I don't impress easily, either. We make a great team, and I'm sure when the gala is over, we will keep in contact."

Imani was downplaying her attraction to Daman, but she didn't want his mother getting the wrong idea. She also wasn't sure if she knew her son was actually competing against her for an estate. His mother was sweet, and her love for her son was evident.

"Mrs. Barker, you raised a remarkable man, and I'm sure the woman Daman decides to settle down with will capture his attention in ways he's never imagined." She cleared her throat before continuing. "Some people are lucky enough to find someone to spend the rest of their lives with, but others have to live with the fact that a fairy-tale ending may not be in their future."

Imani was so caught up in her thoughts that she hadn't noticed that Daman now stood in the entrance of the kitchen. She was unsure of how much he had heard, but whatever he'd heard was more than she had wanted him to know. Apparently, he got the picture because he hastily informed them that he'd fixed a leak in the bathroom and walked back out.

"Imani, I want you to promise me that when my son does finally come to terms with his feelings, you won't turn your back on him. When Daman loves, he loves hard. With him, you have to read between the lines. I know you both have separate lives and say you aren't interested in a relationship, but he's my baby, and I know my son better than he knows himself sometimes."

Imani wasn't sure what to say to Mrs. Barker. She didn't want to upset her. "I can't make any promises, but I'll never intentionally hurt Daman."

Mrs. Barker looked as if she wanted to say more but decided against it.

"I'll get Daman, and we can all sit down and eat."

## Chapter 12

Later that night, Daman lay in his bed thinking about the one woman who seemed to occupy most of his thoughts as of late. It was getting harder to hide his attraction to her, and his mom definitely picked up on his interest today.

During dinner, he had a hard time concentrating on his food, which was something he'd never had a problem with before. He kept wondering about the conversation Imani had with his mother but knew that neither woman would tell him about it. The dinner had been a little tense, and Imani seemed uncomfortable around him. He thought they'd gotten past that, but apparently, he was wrong.

His mom really liked Imani, and it made him feel good inside. He'd caught his mom staring at Imani from time to time with a wishful look in her eyes. Patricia

Barker wouldn't be happy until he was married with children.

He heard the shower turn on and his bathroom door lock. His body was instantly aroused, knowing Imani stood naked on the other side of the door. Dinner had ended two hours ago, and he thought Imani had gone to sleep. He heard the shower curtain open and close and wondered what type of shower gel she used. His question was instantly answered as the scent of vanilla and jasmine seeped under the door, filling his senses. Just imagining her in the shower lathering her body made him ache all over. He should be the one giving her body a good scrub, instead of the loofah she was probably using.

The minute he'd tasted her in Atlanta, he knew he would taste her again. By some he may be deemed as cocky, but to others he was just being truthful. Two people didn't share a kiss that amazing and not have seconds.

Her flavor was imprinted on his tongue, and the look of satisfaction on her face was stamped in his mind. Never had a woman's reaction been so uninhibited with him. She was always so poised, and yet with one flick of his tongue, she became putty in his arms, turning him on in ways that were very new to him.

The water stopped, and he listened to her humming a tune he couldn't quite make out. It had a medium tempo, and he knew he had heard the song on the radio before. It became imperative that he figure out what song she was humming.

Sliding off the bed, he was careful not to make a sound. When he reached the door, he smiled when he recognized the song. It was the old SWV hit, "Weak." He wondered if she was thinking about him when she got out the shower or if she just happened to like that song.

Convincing himself that she had to be thinking about him, he smiled as he made his way back to his bed, tripping over his shoes in the process.

He heard Imani gasp before hearing her bathroom door close again. He didn't mind her quick dash out of the bathroom, but because she had locked his door, he wouldn't be able to go to the bathroom in the middle of the night.

*Suddenly, I have to go to the bathroom.* Daman started to make his way to Imani's room before giving it a second thought.

He lightly knocked and heard some shuffling around on the other side of the door. He assumed she was trying to put on some decent clothes until she opened the door in her towel and motioned for him to come in.

All air gushed out of his lungs as he looked at her. She looked so refreshing and beautiful that for a second, he forgot the excuse he had for bothering her.

"You left my side of the bathroom door locked."

Her eyes widened. "I'm so sorry. I completely forgot."

She went into the bathroom and unlocked his bathroom door. Daman took the brief moment to try to regain his composure. Her towel barely reached midthigh, and her recently washed hair was a mass of curls clipped on top of her head. She looked sexy as hell, and he knew he looked like an idiot staring at her.

"By any chance were you thinking about me when you were humming that SWV tune?"

Her eyes again widened in shock. "You heard me?"

"As a matter of fact, you woke me up. I was sleeping soundly before I heard your sweet voice float through my room."

"I'm sorry. I guess I thought I was being quiet."

He was smiling from ear to ear. She actually believed him. "That's okay, but don't let it happen again."

She put her hands on her hips and adjusted her neck in a way that let him know she was about to rip him a new one. "For your information, I wasn't thinking about you when I was singing, and I was being extremely quiet. You have good hearing if you heard me, but I think you were never asleep in the first place. You probably pressed your ear to the door to hear what I was humming. I heard you trip over something. Were you trying to make your way back to your bed, perhaps?"

The entire time she was talking she kept her voice low so they didn't wake up his mother, but Daman couldn't help it. He laughed a little too loudly when he heard her accurate assessment of the situation.

"I guess we'll never know, but I do think that you should take your hands off your hips while I'm in here. Regardless, you're the reason I had to come to your room since you were the one who locked me out of the bathroom."

"I'll stand however I want to stand when I'm in the room your mother allowed me to stay in." This time she rolled her head, keeping one hand on her hip and pointing a finger at him with the other hand. He recognized the moment she realized her mistake in not obeying him. A man could only take so much.

She attempted to take a step back, but it was too late. He grabbed the arm that was extended and pulled her to him. She gasped at the sudden movement.

"Daman," she said his name as a statement.

"I told you not to stand that way. Now feel what you did."

He grinded his pelvis against her, wanting her to feel the effect she had on him. He expected a smart remark from her, but all she did was stare at him as if she was feeling something she hadn't felt before. Daman usually felt in control, but every time Imani looked at him as if she was trying to figure him out, he lost a little of that control. He prided himself on never allowing a woman to have any power over him, but Imani was turning out to be a woman he could not easily dismiss. She was slowly getting in his system, and he wasn't sure whether he liked that.

He watched her lick her lips as she nodded in understanding.

*Had he spoken out loud?* He knew he hadn't, but she knew what he was thinking, anyway.

"This is insane," he said, this time voicing his thoughts out loud.

"I know," Imani replied breathlessly.

His lips touched hers softly at first, allowing her to get used to the feel of their lips connecting again. He had every intention of controlling the kiss, but once he let go of Imani's arm, she locked her hands across the back of his neck, pulling his tongue deeper into her mouth. The smell of vanilla jasmine mixing with

Imani's natural scent was causing Daman's body to react even more intensely than it had the last time they were together.

His hands expertly roamed her body as she molded herself against him. He wanted to rid her of her towel, but he knew his mom was in the next room, and there was no way he could do the things he wanted to do to her in his mother's house.

He slowly sucked and tugged at her tongue the same way he'd done to her body the last time they were alone. What began as a soft purr turned into an even louder moan as their kiss deepened, taking them to an even higher level of ecstasy. Daman's index finger found its way underneath Imani's towel and touched her sweetness with the perfect amount of pressure for her to let out a soft cry into his mouth. She was slick and wet, and Daman grew even more aroused knowing that he was the cause of her pleasure.

He knew he had to stop while he still had a little sense. When he pulled away, she looked at him with expectant eyes. It was a look he hadn't seen from her before, and all he wanted to do was take her in his arms and hold her. But his desire prevented him from pulling her back to him, knowing that if he did, he wouldn't be able to stop himself again. When he made love to her, he wanted them to be in an unoccupied location, so his mother's home was definitely not an option. The kiss had been explosive. He felt it. She felt it. And the passion never seemed to subside between them. Daman was so wrapped up in his thoughts that he barely registered that Imani had spoken.

"I didn't want this."

He rubbed her cheek with the back of his hand. "Neither did I, but it happened anyway." At least that answer was partially true. From the start, he'd wanted to seduce her. What he hadn't counted on was his need for her growing to such an intense level.

They both fell silent until Imani spoke again.

"This could be disastrous, Daman. As partners in the planning of the gala, we'll only see each other more and more, and what's worse is that we both want something that neither of us is willing to give up."

The real reason they were partners was always looming in the air, but it seemed nothing was very clear to either of them anymore.

"I understand. But it won't go away until we fix the problem. I have a suggestion."

Daman had to choose his next words carefully. He'd never wanted a woman so badly. All they needed was to feed their sexual hunger and ease their curiosity.

"I've known since the moment I met you that I wanted you. I've never had such a strong attraction to a woman before, and I'm man enough to admit that it's your body *and* mind that have me mesmerized. I think if we feed our sexual hunger, we will solve our problem."

In response to the unbroken silence, he continued to talk. "Don't take this the wrong way, but there's a sexual prowess inside you that is dying to break free. I feel it every time we're together. I don't believe the men in your life have handled you the way they should have. They may have satisfied you, but I can fulfill your desires in ways you never imagined. We have chemistry that was evident from the first time we met, so all I'm saying is that it's about time we did something about it. I won't kiss or touch you again until you make the decision. Honestly, the next time we get this intimate, I won't be able to stop."

Daman rubbed his hands over his face before he moved toward the door.

"Daman."

He glanced back at her to see why she'd called his name, and the look he saw in her eyes shocked him. It wasn't anger or fear or apprehension. In her eyes, he saw unreserved lust and a silent understanding that she agreed with everything he said.

"You said you want me, and well, when the time is right, you can have me—all of me. No strings, no obligations and no reservations. You see things in me that no man has ever taken the time to figure out. So yes, I will give you what you want if you promise me one thing."

She stood there facing him, searching his eyes for something. He wasn't sure what she was looking for, so he stood there and let her search. While she searched, he admired the delicate structure of her nose, the adorable way the curls framed her face and the endearing way she crinkled her nose in concentration.

"What do you want me to promise?" he asked when he realized he hadn't responded.

Her eyes suddenly lit, then dimmed. If he hadn't been standing so close to her, he would have missed the flash of acknowledgment in her eyes. He wondered if she'd found what she was searching for.

"Promise me that once the gala is over and the ownership of the estate is settled, we will go our separate ways. We'll look back on this time as a good memory and nothing else."

There was something about the finality of the promise that made him hesitate, but her request seemed simple enough. "Okay. I promise."

## Chapter 13

By early Sunday morning, Imani and Daman were finally leaving Florida after canceling their trip to Georgia. Yesterday, Mrs. Barker's power came back on, but the aftermath of the storm was still very much present.

"I'm so glad you both spent this weekend with me," said Mrs. Barker, hugging Daman before turning to Imani. "Imani, you've been an absolute pleasure."

Imani returned her kind words before hugging the older woman she had instantly taken a liking to.

Before she got into the rental car, Imani pulled a feather out of her purse and said a short prayer to Gamine before releasing the feather into the sky. When she sat down in the car, she realized that Daman had watched her release the feather. Surprisingly, he didn't ask her what she was doing.

Imani adjusted herself in the seat so that they could get comfortable. They were meeting James and the crew at a smaller airport an hour away from the neighborhoods affected by the storm.

"All set?" Daman asked when Imani stopped fidgeting in her seat.

"Yes, I'm ready."

They waved goodbye to Mrs. Barker as the car pulled away from her house. A few minutes into the drive, Imani got a text from Cyd.

"I've been gone all weekend and conveniently, on the day I return, the family decides to have Sunday lunch at my grandfather's house," Imani said with a laugh.

"That seems nice," Daman stated. "I think you will make it to Chicago in plenty of time."

"Yeah, that may be true, but I wanted to go straight home and go to sleep when I got back. We've been traveling a lot lately so I was hoping for a little R & R." Imani loved being around her family, but they could be exhausting at times. Especially when she'd been MIA ever since she was on the radio. She wanted to avoid any Daman-related topics. She texted Cyd and asked how many people were planning to attend. Cyd responded within seconds.

"Oh, man," Imani said aloud. "She said at least fifty people are planning to be there."

"Fifty people," Daman said in surprise. "I thought you said this was a lunch."

"It is a lunch, but my grandfather is very well-known in Naperville so many people in the neighborhood tend to get invited. Even the last minute events like this one spread like wildfire."

Imani's cell phone vibrated. "Cyd said Taheim and Jaleen will both be there."

Daman's hearty laugh filled the car. "I was going to go to Detroit after we dropped you off, but I think I may want to check out that barbecue instead."

Imani hadn't seen most of her family since her appearance on *The Jimmy King Morning Show*. There was no doubt that they'd be the main topic of conversation.

"Of course, since I invited myself, I don't have to go," Daman said as he kept his eyes on the road while occasionally stealing glances her way.

"No, it's fine," Imani said. "I think you'll enjoy yourself. But be forewarned, my family is a little overwhelming at times. I know they probably all listened to the show so you should expect a couple questions to be thrown your way."

Four hours later, they arrived outside of the Burrstone household in Naperville, Illinois. Judging from the number of double-parked cars on the narrow street, a lot of people were already there.

As they were walking toward the house, Imani stopped in her tracks when she heard a familiar laugh.

"Is everything okay?" Daman asked.

Imani couldn't answer right away, not until she found the person who had laughed.

"And so the saga begins…" she said, as her suspicions were confirmed and Cyd rounded the corner of the house.

Daman followed the direction of Imani's gaze. He squinted his eyes as he looked from the woman to Imani. "Is that your sister?"

"Yes, that's her. And if I'm not mistaken, the rest of the clan isn't far behind."

**KIMANI™ ROMANCE**

# An Important Message from the Publisher

Dear Reader,

Because you've chosen to read one of our fine novels, I'd like to say "thank you"! And, as a special way to say thank you, I'm offering to send you two more Kimani™ Romance novels and two surprise gifts— absolutely FREE! These books will keep it real with true-to-life African American characters that turn up the heat and sizzle with passion.

Please enjoy the free books and gifts with our compliments...

*Glenda Howard*
For Kimani Press™

*Peel off Seal and Place Inside...*

K-ROM-13B

# THE EDITOR'S "THANK YOU" FREE GIFTS INCLUDE:

➤ Two Kimani™ Romance Novels
➤ Two exciting surprise gifts

YES! I have placed my Editor's "thank you" Free Gifts seal in the space provided at right. Please send me 2 FREE Books, and my 2 FREE Mystery Gifts. I understand that I am under no obligation to purchase anything further, as explained on the back of this card.

PLACE FREE GIFTS SEAL HERE

## 168/368 XDL FV32

*Please Print*

FIRST NAME

LAST NAME

ADDRESS

APT.#

CITY

STATE/PROV.

ZIP/POSTAL CODE

## Thank You!

Offer limited to one per household and not applicable to series that subscriber is currently receiving.

**Your Privacy**—The Harlequin® Reader Service is committed to protecting your privacy. Our Privacy Policy is available online at www.ReaderService.com or upon request from the Harlequin Reader Service. We make a portion of our mailing list available to reputable third parties that offer products we believe may interest you. If you prefer that we not exchange your name with third parties, or if you wish to clarify or modify your communication preferences, please visit us at www.ReaderService.com/consumerchoice or write to us at Harlequin Reader Service Preference Service, P.O. Box 9062, Buffalo, NY 14269. Include your complete name and address.

# ✦ HARLEQUIN® READER SERVICE—Here's How It Works:

Accepting your 2 free books and 2 free gifts (gifts valued at approximately $10.00) places you under no obligation to buy anything. You may keep the books and gifts and return the shipping statement marked "cancel." If you do not cancel, about a month later we'll send you 4 additional books and bill you just $5.19 each in the U.S. or $5.49 each in Canada. That is a savings of at least 20% off the cover price. Shipping and handling is just 50¢ per book in the U.S. and 75¢ per book in Canada.* You may cancel at any time, but if you choose to continue, every month we'll send you 4 more books, which you may either purchase at the discount price or return to us and cancel your subscription.

*Terms and prices subject to change without notice. Prices do not include applicable taxes. Sales tax applicable in N.Y. Canadian residents will be charged applicable taxes. Offer not valid in Quebec. All orders subject to credit approval. Credit or debit balances in a customer's account(s) may be offset by any other outstanding balance owed by or to the customer. Offer available while quantities last. Books received may not be as shown. Please allow 4 to 6 weeks for delivery.

**BUSINESS REPLY MAIL**

FIRST-CLASS MAIL    PERMIT NO. 717    BUFFALO, NY

POSTAGE WILL BE PAID BY ADDRESSEE

**HARLEQUIN READER SERVICE**
PO BOX 1867
BUFFALO NY 14240-9952

NO POSTAGE
NECESSARY
IF MAILED
IN THE
UNITED STATES

If offer card is missing write to: Harlequin Reader Service, P.O. Box 1867, Buffalo, NY 14240-1867 or visit www.ReaderService.com

Just as she finished those words, Lex and Mya headed in their direction.

Imani leaned over and whispered to Daman. "Be prepared, because they are definitely going to ask you a lot of questions."

As the women approached, Imani introduced Daman to Cyd, Mya and Lex. Taheim and Jaleen arrived soon after. Then, the "welcome crew" got an earful from Imani. "Y'all have a lot of explaining to do. I can't believe that at our age you're still scheming."

Imani didn't appreciate the chuckles from the group.

Taheim jumped in before Imani could get started on them again. "Well, if the two of you didn't work so hard, you would have noticed that we all know each other. Although I must say that I'm kind of glad you didn't. *The Jimmy King Morning Show* was pretty interesting."

Once again, everyone laughed at her expense. Imani felt Daman's eyes on her, but she refused to look at him.

"One of you could have told me how well you knew Imani when I told you her name during our meeting," Daman said to Taheim and Jaleen.

Taheim decided to answer again. "You two didn't kill each other, so it seems the plan worked."

Imani dared to look at Daman, as Daman glared at Taheim. Sensing Imani's eyes on him, Daman turned toward her, with an unreadable expression on his face. But in an instant, it turned to one of clear understanding. She got it, too. *They wanted us to get to know each other on a more personal level.* His eyes dropped down to her lips. Her lips parted as if they had a mind of their own, inviting him for another sample. Jaleen cleared his throat. All eyes were on them as Imani and Daman turned back to the group.

*Why do I let this man affect me?* Imani couldn't believe that even in front of their friends, they couldn't deny the chemistry.

Cyd spoke up. "Imani, Grandpa Burrstone wants to discuss the barbecue with us. Can we steal you away from Daman for a moment?"

Cyd was trying to bait her, but Imani refused. The annual Burrstone barbecue was an event that her grandfather loved to throw every year. The Burrstones were a big pillar in the Chicago community so for the past few years, her grandfather recruited the assistance of his granddaughters, owners of Elite Events Incorporated.

Daman glanced at Imani, and she tried her best to keep a solemn face. "Yes, I can spare some time."

"Great!" Cyd exclaimed with enthusiasm as she grabbed Imani's arm. Mya and Lex followed.

"Okay, I get first dibs," Cyd said to Lex and Mya as they sat in the parked car. She clasped her hands in her lap and looked at Imani, ready to open up the proverbial can of worms. "Sis, I think it was a great idea that we didn't tell you Daman was Taheim and Jaleen's new partner."

Imani started to speak, but Cyd shushed her.

"Before you say anything, I'm also glad you and Daman were on *The Jimmy King Morning Show* together. As far as your and Daman's private conversation being heard by many listeners, well, that's your fault."

"And Daman's," Mya added with a giggle.

"Tell me something, sis, was it good? Because I know you hit that."

Imani's mouth dropped open, and all the women laughed at the surprised look on her face.

"Come off that snotty attitude, girl," Lex said. "We know you aren't shocked. And you're not shy, either. You like sex just as much as the rest of us. Now man up, and give us some details."

"Hell, yeah," Mya added. "Back in the day, you'd make us give you all the details on our boyfriends, dates…"

"…and mistakes," Lex interrupted with a smile.

They nodded their heads in agreement.

"I know, but that was different."

"How's that?" Cyd asked.

Imani thought carefully before answering the question. "That was the old me, over five years ago. I'm older, wiser and not the romantic I used to be."

Mya grunted. "You know what I think?"

"No, but you're going to tell me, anyway."

"I think that for once since Gamine's death, you met a man you can't ignore. You always dismiss men and keep your feelings guarded, but clearly Daman is breaking through those walls."

"You're one to talk, Mya! Neither of you can say anything about how I handle Daman because you're all just as bad as I am. Plus, I have to keep the estate in mind at all times. I refuse to get played."

"But this isn't about us. This is about you," Lex chimed in.

"And why are you so concerned about getting played when you claim you don't even like him?" Cyd persisted.

Once again, Cyd was trying to bait her into opening up. She wondered how much she should tell them and decided that she could talk to her close friends about anything.

"Okay, so here's the thing, Cyd. I did not hit that. Not even close."

The sighs heard in the car proved they weren't expecting that answer.

"Ugh, okay, I'm lying a little bit. I've never slept with Daman, but we have come close several times."

"Now that's more like it. Continue," Cyd exclaimed.

"Well, each time we get close to having sex, he stops right before it happens. He says he can tell that I'm still trying to process what's happening between us, and until I do, he's not going to initiate anything else. The ball is in my court."

"Do you find it hard to resist him?" Mya asked.

Imani did her best to give her a *what-do-you-think* look because as her best friend, Mya knew the answer but wanted her to admit it, anyway.

"If I did think it was easy to resist him, would we be having this conversation? I'm only human, and he's sexy as hell."

Mya just smiled.

"Every time we get together, I feel like my old self. Even though we haven't taken our relationship any further, the intimate moments we have had have been so special that it makes me question any intimacy I've had up to this point. It's almost on a whole other level of lust."

Imani thought about the time she'd shared with Daman. How he made her feel. How comfortable she felt with him. She was so caught up in her thoughts that she was unaware of the three sets of eyes watching her face with knowing expressions.

"Oh, you have definitely got it bad," Lex said with a giggle.

"Am I that transparent?"

"Yes!" all three women practically shouted. They all burst out laughing.

Imani looked over at Cyd. "How about we go back to the house and stop talking about me."

"Whatever you say, sis," Cyd said, as she opened the car door. "But one last question. What are you going to do about your feelings for Daman?"

"I don't know. Since the ball's in my court, I figure now is a great time to try and work on controlling myself whenever I'm around him."

The looks on their faces showed disbelief, but Imani didn't care what they thought. She knew how to control her body, although that wasn't exactly apparent when she was in the presence of Daman Barker.

As the women began making their way back to the house, Imani noticed Daman standing on the side of the house, talking with some people from the neighborhood. She stopped watching him long enough to respond to a question Lex had asked. When she turned back to Daman, he was staring right at her. The look in his eyes showed a hunger that only she could fill. She swallowed the lump in her throat and practically begged her eyes to look away.

*Please stay in control. Body, don't fail me now.*

Cyd spoke, fueling the fire, while glancing from Daman to Imani.

"Well, sis, you may think you can keep your relationship strictly professional, but your eyes are saying something different. I've never seen you act this way around a man before."

Imani used Cyd as an excuse to tear her eyes away from Daman. "I know. I have to do something about him."

"Or do something to him! Come on, what's wrong with you? You need to lighten up about Daman. Your control issues are really starting to bug me," Cyd said with a laugh. "Some words of advice, big sis. Don't overthink it, and don't try to control how you feel or think you can control how he feels. When it comes to the heart, it's unpredictable."

"I feel you, Cyd, but Daman isn't just any man."

"You're right. He's the one man you haven't tried to completely dismiss…the one who's gotten under your skin."

"Look who's talking…queen of dismissing her loyal followers."

"Why must you always make me sound stuck-up? I'm selective. There's a difference. Most men can't handle me, anyway."

Both women giggled, knowing that with Cyd, even the men who did try, failed. Imani stared at her younger sister in admiration. Somewhere along the way, they had switched roles on giving advice.

"Since when do you counsel people on matters of the heart?"

"I don't know. I just worry about you sometimes, and I like the changes I see in you since you started working with Daman. You seem to have a little of your old self back, and that makes me happy."

And with that comment, Cyd made her way to the house. Taking one final glance toward Daman, Imani followed behind Cyd. She was less than thrilled about the next hour or so, and she knew that the parents and elders were going to make her the main topic of conversation.

*Imani was right,* Daman thought as he finished up a conversation with the fifteenth person who'd asked him about his relationship with Imani. He almost regretted his decision to come to the lunch. They shouldn't even call it a lunch because it was more like a party.

But despite being under the eye of scrutiny, he had really enjoyed getting to know Imani's parents. Mr. Rayne had a sarcastic sense of humor and joked about the way Daman was looking at Imani. Mrs. Rayne had a very warm personality and was full of compliments for both her daughters.

Throughout the entire night, Daman stole glances at Imani. *What did she expect when she was constantly dipping her tongue out to moisten her lips?* As it always seemed to go with them, she caught him staring each and every time. And every time, she only smiled, causing him to wonder what she was thinking.

Mostly everyone was in the house now, so he found an empty bench in the backyard. He should have been counting how many times he said *we're just friends* today. And he'd heard Imani's name being called the most out of everyone in attendance. Not because of him, but because they needed her for something. If some food ran out, they called her to see if they should order more. If some younger kids were acting too rowdy, they called Imani to calm them down. If someone wanted to know about specific details regarding the annual Burrstone barbecue, they asked Imani, even though there were three other members from Elite Events present.

"No wonder why the woman's exhausted," Daman said aloud to himself.

"I agree, my grandbaby works too hard," Mr. Burrstone said as he approached Daman. "Mind if I join you?"

"Not at all, sir," Daman answered as he pondered how Mr. Burrstone knew he was talking about Imani. He'd been introduced to Imani's grandfather earlier, but they hadn't talked much.

"I keep telling Imani that she needs to slow down. Then I see how much the family relies on her, and I know it's not possible."

"Why isn't it possible?" Daman asked. To him, it appeared to be an easy fix. Everyone needed to start relying on someone else other than Imani.

Mr. Burrstone glanced at Daman before responding. "You know, Imani's a lot like her grandmother was at her age. And her mother. Vibrant. Full of life. Women like my wife, daughter and granddaughter take on the weight of their family in exchange for nothing at all. Feisty as all get out, but don't let them fool you." Mr. Burrstone laughed as he crossed his arms over his chest. "You see, son, the reason I say it isn't possible is because it's in her blood. Imani was programmed that way. It may not be fair and she may not always be able to handle her responsibilities, whether they are her responsibilities or others'. But she will never stop caring or being so involved because she was meant to be just who she is."

Mr. Burrstone's views were very old school, yet they made sense to Daman. But he still didn't think the responsibilities and burdens of a family should fall on one person.

"I still think there is a way she could balance everything without getting so exhausted."

Mr. Burrstone laughed again. "I agree with you, Daman. And maybe one day, she'll figure that out."

With that said, Mr. Burrstone got up and walked away. As Daman stayed seated on that bench, thinking about what Mr. Burrstone had said, he wondered if there was a way he could help her figure out how to balance everything.

"Hey, man, where are you?" Jaleen asked as he waved his hand in front of Daman's face. "You're thinking about Imani, aren't you?" Jaleen sat on the bench next to Daman.

"Yeah, man. I don't know what it is about that woman that has me so twisted. Today, she was a different person than I'd seen before. I liked seeing her around her family."

"I knew she would stay on your mind from the minute you first mentioned her name. So did Taheim."

"Yeah, I know. She could be a real problem for me."

"Yes, she could. Imani is the type you marry, not the type you bed, and a lot of us are pretty protective of her. She's been through a lot over the years, and no one wants to see her get hurt. Get it?"

Daman hadn't missed the tone in his friend's voice. It was obvious he was looking out for her best interest. "Yeah, I get it, and that's the main reason why I wouldn't try anything with her."

Jaleen gave him a look of disbelief, and Daman 'fessed up.

"Okay, so I have tried something, but what I mean is that I would never intentionally hurt her. Truthfully though, I want that estate, and the only thing standing in my way is Imani."

"Why is that estate so important to you, anyway?"

"I promised my dad I would buy the estate when the Simses decided to sell. If it was important enough for him to ask me to do that, I want to make sure I follow his wishes. That's all."

Jaleen nodded his head in understanding, but Daman felt he had to go a little further with his explanation. "Man, Jay, trust me. I wish I weren't competing against Imani. It's hard to control myself around her sometimes. It's cool when we're talking business about the gala. And even then, I'm completely aware of everything about her. But it's even worse when we're alone. I purposely don't get to know a lot about any female I mess with, but from the first day I met Imani, I learned more about her than I wanted to. Now, after meeting her family, and Imani meeting my mom, I still want to learn more about her."

Daman stopped talking when he felt Jaleen watching him closely. Jaleen knew a lot about Daman's history with women, and it didn't take a genius to figure out that he didn't have a clue about how to handle Imani.

"D, we can't always control who we fall for or why we fall for that person."

"I'm not falling for her. I'm just a little curious… that's all."

Jaleen laughed, and Daman couldn't help but laugh along.

"Whatever, man. All I'm saying is that you got some thinking to do. And now that you've met the Burrstones, you know you have to go to their annual barbecue—especially since Mrs. Rayne personally invited you."

"Yeah, I know. And I don't mind going to the barbecue. But as far as Imani's concerned, I'll just wait and see what happens. You know me, man. I'm not putting that much thought into my feelings." He'd already told Jaleen way more than he'd planned on telling him.

"Anyway, what happened in the office while I was out?"

Daman had a lot of thinking to do, and luckily, Jaleen picked up on his clues and dropped the subject. He hadn't made any plans with Imani in the coming weeks, so he'd use that time to get his head on straight.

## Chapter 14

Imani weaved through occupied tables as she made her way to an empty spot in the corner of her favorite coffee shop.

She took a sip of her caramel macchiato, savoring the sweet taste as she waited for Cyd, Mya and Lex to arrive. She was meeting with the girls for a much-needed shopping trip and was the first to arrive.

The annual barbecue was slowly approaching, and she hadn't seen Daman for a few weeks. Earlier that day, her mother had informed her that she invited Daman to the barbecue. Even though they hadn't spoken to each other since returning from Florida, they had both talked to Vicky and the volunteers for the gala on conference calls at least three times a week. Everything was running smoothly, and Imani wondered why the Simses even needed their help when Vicky, Pete and the students were apparently very capable of planning the gala without them.

As she took a sip of her warm drink, she tried to push Daman out of her mind. She hated the fact that she allowed him to dominate so many of her thoughts. She couldn't deny that she missed being around him. The proposition he gave her at his mother's house seemed reasonable, considering their strong attraction to each other. She had thought that all she would need was a couple of weeks to reprocess the situation and decide that an affair with Daman wasn't worth it. That didn't work. The longer they were apart, the more she wanted to say yes to him. The only thing she confirmed in their time apart was that an affair with a man like Daman was exactly what she needed. She had to get him out of her system no matter how short their affair would be. He'd proved that he could definitely deliver in the bedroom...if given the chance.

Her iPhone rang, disrupting her thoughts. She quickly glanced at her screen before answering.

"Hello, Vicky. Is everything okay?"

"I'm afraid that I have some last-minute news that needs immediate attention. I received a phone call from one of our biggest sponsors for the gala, Mr. and Mrs. Walsh. In this economy, everyone is suffering and the Walshes sound unsure about sponsoring any events this year. They are good people, but they like to have their butts kissed every now and then. I need you and Daman to go visit them at their home in St. Simons Island, Georgia. They're having a brunch with some of Atlanta's finest so it would really be great if you both could attend on behalf of the staff."

Imani instantly felt a little excited by the thought of seeing Daman again.

"Sure. Have you talked to Daman?"

"No, I called you first. The brunch is this Saturday. Would that be a problem?"

Imani promptly searched through her planner. "No, that won't be a problem."

"Great, I'll call Daman now."

"Thanks, Vicky. I'll give Daman a call in about ten minutes, after you tell him about the meeting."

As Imani hung up the phone, her thoughts drifted back to Daman. She knew he would be receptive to the affair, but that fact didn't make her any less nervous about approaching the subject. Her phone rang again. She answered without glancing at the screen, figuring it was Cyd, Mya, or Lex.

"Are you close by?"

"Well, that depends. Where are you? If you want me close by, I can make it happen."

Imani froze at the sound of the deep, enticing voice on the other end of the line.

"Hi, Daman. Sorry, I thought you were someone else. Did you talk to Vicky?"

"Actually, I did. That's why I'm calling. I didn't mean to catch you at a bad time. Vicky told me that you were free to meet with Mr. and Mrs. Walsh, as well."

"Yes, I'm free. So I guess we better book our flights."

"No need. We can take my jet, if that's okay with you."

"Yes, that's fine with me. It will give us a chance to discuss the gala more."

Imani saw the ladies enter the coffee shop and make

their way to the front counter to order. She continued to discuss the weekend plans with Daman for a few more minutes until the ladies had their pastries and coffee in hand.

"Sorry to cut this conversation short, but I have to wrap up a few things before tomorrow, and my company just got here. Thanks for calling."

"No problem."

As the women approached, Cyd and Lex gave Imani a quick hug. Mya just looked at Imani questioningly. "Why do you look so anxious? Was that phone call bad news?"

"Nope."

Imani knew she had answered Mya's question a little too quickly.

"Oh, really? That wouldn't happen to have been Daman, would it? I heard he was coming to the barbecue."

"Don't you all have anything better to do than get in my business?"

Mya and Lex glanced at Cyd before they all answered with a solid no.

Imani shook her head. "Anyway, Daman and I have to leave for Georgia soon on business regarding the gala. We'll only be gone this weekend."

The look on Cyd's face was one of doubt.

"I'm serious, Cyd. It's only business."

"If you say so, sis."

"Okay, let's get this day moving," Lex chimed in. "I'm ready for some shopping."

As the ladies ate and discussed the stores they would check out, Imani tried her best to get Daman out of her mind. Unfortunately, the more she tried, the more her head hurt. She closed her eyes tightly and tilted her head sideways so that the sun from the window could beam on her face. She was definitely in for a long day.

Daman returned to his home office after ending his call with Imani. He looked over at Malik, the private investigator, who was patiently waiting for all the information he had given Daman to sink in.

"Embezzlement! Are you sure that this is correct? Are all these accounts false?" Daman asked as he flipped through a couple pages. He refused to believe that his uncle would set up false customer accounts so he could pocket the money they'd received from several investors and top clients.

"Yes, I'm sure. My inside source proved that your uncle falsified your signature on plenty of dirty documents for these accounts."

Daman rubbed his temple and let out a long and ragged breath. "How is that possible? I wasn't vice president when Barker Architecture reached out to our investors in 2008."

Malik grew quiet and took out several more documents. "Frank still continues to gather money from a couple investors. Gathering from the timeline, it seems that he started covering his tracks more when you began questioning him about misleading financial documents. That's where the trail gets fuzzy."

Daman was having a hard time accepting his uncle's actions. After his father's death, his uncle took on his role as father. How could his uncle jeopardize the company and steal from trusted investors and clients?

"That's not all," Malik said as he pulled out one more packet of documents from his briefcase. "I have a list of people that I'm investigating who invested money in Barker Architecture. I have a feeling your uncle is acting alone, but just in case he isn't, I need to rule out other options."

Malik handed Daman the first few sheets of the packet. Daman scanned over the list noticing a few familiar names, shareholders and clients. His eyes stopped short when he got to a name he definitely didn't expect to see on the list.

"Edward Burrstone?" Daman asked Malik. "That's Imani's grandfather. Why is his name on this list?"

"He's an investor, but it took me a while to find him. He isn't listed as Edward Burrstone on any of the paperwork." Malik handed him the last part of the packet. "After a lot of digging, I found out that the name he used when investing in Barker Architecture was Paul John Taylor."

Daman shook his head in acknowledgment. "I've seen that name before." He handed the paperwork back to Malik. "What does all this mean?"

"It means the case is going well and I'm gathering enough evidence to prove that your uncle is guilty of investment fraud. As far as the shareholders, I see no reason for you to worry or believe that they were aware of your uncle embezzling money."

"I hope not," Daman replied, still reeling over the idea that Edward Burrstone was a key investor in the company.

Malik placed his paperwork in his briefcase as he stood to leave. Gripping Daman's shoulders, Malik

gave his best pep talk to ensure that Daman understood he was doing the right thing.

Daman had spent most of Thursday night bothered
by the possibility that his uncle was facing some serious jail time when everything came to light. He'd barely
slept and had only worked a half day at R&W because
of his flight to Georgia. He glanced at the clock in his
hotel room and hurried to hop in the shower because
he was due to pick up Imani in an hour. Although he
was looking forward to seeing her again, he was worried that his bad mood might affect their time together.

As he stepped out of the shower and into his adjoining bedroom, he briefly wondered what Imani was
doing, and if she was just getting out of the shower, too.
He wondered who she had met with the day before and
instantly tensed when he thought about it being another
man. He'd spent the past few weeks wondering how,
after all this time, he'd found a woman who made him
think about her even when she wasn't around. He wasn't
sure if he liked that. He knew he couldn't treat her like
the other women he dated, which was easy because he
respected her too much. But there was something in
the way she looked at him that made him want to open
up and tell her everything. He'd already shared more
with her than any woman in his past.

He was quickly regretting the promise he made to
her that he wouldn't make the next move without her
permission. He cursed under his breath at his stupidity.
He knew she wanted him as badly as he wanted her,
but Imani thought too much about the consequences
of her actions. He felt like it was his job to help push

her toward making the right decision. And in this case, the right decision was engaging in an explosive affair with yours truly.

His doorbell rang, signifying that his driver was there to take him to pick up Imani. They made it to her condo in record time, considering that Chicago traffic was always congested.

As Daman entered the complex, the guard told him Imani was expecting him and let him go up. He'd barely knocked when she opened the door.

"Good morning, Daman. I'm ready."

"Great. The car is downstairs. Let me get your luggage."

"Thank you."

As Daman reached out for Imani's luggage, he noticed how casual she looked in her black-and-pink jogging outfit and gym shoes. She looked calm and relaxed. Her face was free of makeup and her hair was pulled into a high ponytail. She looked a lot younger, almost innocent, with her hair styled that way.

She glanced up at him and smiled that sexy smile of hers as if she knew he needed to see it to forget about his hellish evening. Seeing her, his good mood was instantly restored. Strangely enough, he wished she did hold all the answers. Hell, it would definitely make his life a whole lot easier. Unfortunately, his phone vibrated, disrupting the moment. It was a text message from Malik:

My inside source received new information. We'll be able to close this case soon. We can talk more when you get back to Chicago.

Daman quickly replied, *"Okay,"* and turned back toward Imani. Just like that, his bad mood was back.

"Let's get this show on the road," he said, not caring if his voice sounded aggravated.

## Chapter 15

The jet ride was long and confusing for Imani. She had no idea why Daman was in such a foul mood. He was avoiding eye contact, but she'd seen the desire in his eyes when she'd first met him this morning. Bad mood or not, she refused to be ignored the entire trip.

She got him to discuss some gala plans for all of twenty minutes before he went mute again. And even after they landed and got into the car sent by the Walshes, he remained silent.

In her peripheral vision, she could see him adjusting himself in his seat, tugging on his jeans and rubbing his temple. That man made every simple act look erotic without even trying. But he was clearly stressed, and it didn't have anything to do with her.

*I wonder what that text was about...*

Whatever it was, it couldn't have been good news. When he finally glanced her way, she started to look away, but his sad eyes held her hostage. He didn't say anything. Instead, his eyes dropped down to her lips and lingered there for a while.

He licked his lips, causing her eyes to drop down to his mouth, as well, only her eyes didn't stay there. She openly admired his physical features, daring to be as bold as Daman. They'd observed each other before; however, the more their relationship grew, the bolder their stares became.

Imani watched as Daman's chest heaved slowly to the rhythmic beat of his heart and instantly realized that her breathing matched his. Millions of questions were floating around in her head. *How could one person affect you so much that your breathing begins to equal theirs?*

She could only imagine how in tune they would be if they actually explored a physical relationship, especially if they felt this connected in a car. She wondered if it was possible to take the next step in their professional relationship, cater to their physical needs and still plan the gala as if nothing had happened. She wasn't sure if Daman still felt the same way, but she knew she'd given up on ignoring the obvious.

She inched a little closer and leaned into him to whisper words she didn't want the driver to hear. "Consider this my permission to allow you to make the next move. Let's talk about bringing our relationship to the next level."

Daman shuddered as she spoke, and Imani giggled because she knew his ears were his weak spot. A quick look into his eyes proved he was still thinking about something.

"After the way I've been treating you today, I owe you an explanation."

Imani smiled. Not exactly the response she was looking for, but she appreciated his honesty. "Okay. What's been going on?"

Daman inhaled deeply. "I received some really bad news about Barker Architecture, and I didn't want to take my anger out on you."

She understood his decision to remain quiet, although she was the type of person that talked situations out, rather than holding in all her feelings. She wanted to ask Daman what the bad news was about, but she didn't want to put him in a difficult spot. She'd learned he was rather private with personal issues.

"I understand, and I hate to hear that you received bad news. If you need to talk about it, I'm a good listener."

He seemed to appreciate her offer. "Thanks, I appreciate that."

It grew silent once again, but Imani no longer saw sadness in Daman's eyes. It had been replaced with a longing that she realized had to do with her.

The car slowed down and turned onto a winding road, leading to an enormous house adjacent to a beautiful beach. Imani was consumed by the splendor of her surroundings. She didn't know that Georgia had such amazing beaches. Tearing her eyes away from the beautiful scenery, she met Daman's gaze. She'd given him the green light to engage in a sexual relationship with her, yet the intensity in his look still unnerved her. It was a look that only Daman could give, a promise that he would collect on her offer.

The car came to a stop and the driver opened the car door to let them out.

"Welcome to Walsh Manor," said a man dressed in an all-black butler uniform. "I will be taking you on a quick tour of the grounds and show you where you will both be staying. While you're here, the staff can get you anything you need. Since it's now 5:30 p.m., Mr. and Mrs. Walsh will meet with you both in the morning so you can rest before brunch tomorrow."

The butler motioned for them to follow him. As they made their way up the stairs of the mansion, Imani was astounded by how large Walsh Manor actually was.

"Any chance you can relax and treat this as a mini vacation?" Daman whispered. "I promise to make it worth the trip. I've been craving to taste you again, and now seems perfect since you just accepted my offer."

Imani stared at Daman, baffled by how he could make something so erotic sound so nonchalant. "You say that as if anything we do will be as simple as drinking coffee in the morning."

"My, my. You didn't learn anything, did you?"

"Well, you haven't learned anything, either, because you continue to talk to me as if I can't have you eating out the palm of my hand."

Daman thought about her comment for a minute. "On second thought, I think I taught you a little too well if you're talking to me like this, Miss Prim and Proper."

Imani hit Daman on the shoulder, causing him to yelp. "You're going to pay for calling me that. My thoughts right now are anything but prim and proper."

"Oh, I like it when you talk dirty."

"Shall we begin the tour?" the butler asked from a few feet ahead of them. They nodded in agreement.

Their bags were placed on a rolling cart. "They will be delivered to your rooms."

They entered a front screen room and the butler led Imani and Daman through a set of swinging white doors leading outside to the gated yard. Her nose was instantly greeted with the combination of sweetness from the flowers and the saltiness of the ocean. Imani and Daman were speechless as they walked through the path of trees leading to an open garden of beautiful flowers and striking plants that overlooked the ocean.

"This is amazing," Imani said softly, as she admired the beautiful scenery.

When the butler turned to answer a question Daman had asked, she quickly made her way to the edge of the water and pulled a feather out of her pocket. As she held up her hand and released the feather, she watched it catch in the wind and drift away.

Staring out at the never-ending ocean was extremely relaxing, but a quickening of her heart made her turn around. She saw Daman glance away and continue to follow the butler up a winding path through the garden. He'd seen her release a feather several times and hadn't asked her anything, but she knew his curiosity would eventually get the best of him. She caught up with them as they approached a small beach house at the end of the path.

"For the length of your stay, Mr. and Mrs. Walsh ask that you both make yourselves comfortable in their guest beach house. Everything you need can be found inside. There's also a list of important phone numbers located next to every phone."

Usually Imani would have asked for a separate accommodation to have her privacy, but lately, she realized that no matter where she stayed, Daman was always close by.

"Thank you for the warm hospitality."

"Yes, your hospitality is appreciated," Daman stated after Imani.

"You're both welcome. I will have someone bring over your luggage. Here are the keys." The butler handed them each a pair and walked back to the main house.

Imani opened the door, and Daman followed her inside. The two-level beach house was inviting and cozy. It was decorated with Caribbean-style art pieces and furniture. There was a fully equipped kitchen, dining room and living room. There was also one bedroom on each level, with its own bathroom. Even though they were technically stationed in a backyard, the beach house made her feel extremely secluded.

Imani glanced out the front window and noticed that she couldn't even see Walsh Manor from the beach house. The only views from the front windows were of the garden and ocean. Daman hugged her from behind as he glanced out that same window. It felt natural for her to rest her head on his shoulder and lean into his hug. She knew if she wasn't careful, she could fall for this man.

Imani turned around to face Daman and slowly wrapped her arms around his neck. For what seemed like the hundredth time since they'd first been introduced, she wondered why her body reacted to his touch, even when he was barely touching her. It was as if her body knew the exact moment he would touch her and was prepared for the electric sparks she felt every time.

Daman smiled, only this was a smile she'd never seen before. It was rugged and sexy in that untamed-man-of-the-jungle sort of way.

"You're not having second thoughts, are you?"

She was too wrapped up in their embrace to fully register his question. "Far from it," she replied, as she tilted her head and parted her lips as an invitation for him to sample her again.

Daman took the hint, and in one swift move, his lips were on hers, exploring her mouth with the same urgency that she felt. Instantly, her stomach did flip-flops as she felt his tongue slide in and out of her mouth. He kissed her as if they'd kissed thousands of times before, and the thought that she felt so connected to him made her sigh into his mouth.

Daman managed to reach a part of her that she often kept closed to the opposite sex. He was beginning to break down all of her barriers, and instead of being afraid of the fact that they were getting so close so fast, she was excited. Until the gala was over, she would allow herself to enjoy Daman's company and the emotions he awakened inside her. If only for a short while, she would know what it felt like to give in to her desires.

Neither heard the constant knocking at the door until the person decided to ask if anyone was inside. Daman groaned as he went to answer the door to quickly gather their luggage.

Imani's stomach growled, and she knew she should

eat something, but she didn't want to mess up the mood by stuffing her face. They'd spent the majority of the day traveling and touring the mansion and garden, without taking time to eat. Unfortunately, the growling didn't let up, and soon she realized that Daman's stomach was growling, as well.

"Maybe we should eat something," Imani suggested reluctantly.

"That sounds like a plan. The cabinets and fridge are stocked with food. I'm sure we can whip something up quickly. Besides, we'll both need the energy."

She shivered as she turned to follow Daman into the kitchen. Looking through the cabinets, they decided to make a quick southern dish. They moved easily in the kitchen as if they'd cooked together all their lives. They were able to finish dinner in record time.

"Your family relies on you a lot."

Imani looked up from her plate. "Yes, I know."

Daman hesitated for a while as if he wanted to ask more, and she felt his watchful eyes analyzing her. It was crazy how the same eyes that often drove her insane with passion were also ones that sometimes drove her insane with anxiety.

"Do you ever think it's unfair that your family turns to you for everything, even though other people are capable of doing what you do?"

Imani drew in a soft breath, wondering why Daman would bring up something so random. There were very few people who knew the responsibility she felt when it came to her family. Strangely, she wanted to be honest with Daman, knowing that if she lied, he would probably know, anyway.

"Gamine was more than the matriarch of our family. She was our heart and soul. I've always been family oriented and wanted what was best for everyone. It didn't matter to me that being so involved with family was a large responsibility. I know that we don't live forever, but it never occurred to me that she wouldn't be here. I still don't think I've found a balance between being my own person and trying to embody some of Gamine's character, but I'm working on it."

Daman tilted his head and leaned toward Imani, who was sitting opposite him at the table. "How long have you been trying to find a happy balance?"

"Ever since Gamine passed away. My grandfather always says that individuals are born into certain roles and must accept their place in the family. When Gamine passed away, I had no choice but to be strong for my family. I'd never seen my mother so lost, and even though my father remained strong, the loss was unbearable for him at times, too. My sister, who is usually my main source of comfort, didn't even know what to do with herself, and that went for the rest of the family, as well. When everything in your life seems to be going well, you never imagine being in a situation where no one can help because everyone is at such a loss. So I decided not to let that happen. I decided to be the rock for my family...like Gamine would have been."

"Imani, people need to grieve. You can't take on the weight of the world or hold back your feelings because in the end, no one loses but you."

"I know that, and although I tell myself that all the time, it's hard to break a habit."

Daman got up from the table and sat beside Imani.

"Maybe you never really allowed yourself to grieve."

"Maybe I didn't. I used to think I'd have all the answers when I became an adult. In reality, I never have all the answers."

Daman was quiet as he gathered his thoughts. "Being adults doesn't mean we need to have all the answers. When my father passed away, I learned that you can't control everything, and unexpected tragedies are bound to happen. I haven't figured it all out, either, and I spend the majority of my life glossing over my accomplishments, always pushing for something greater. My dad was so amazing, and I always knew I had to live up to my potential. He left a legacy, and I want to leave one, too."

Imani slowly stroked Daman's hand to offer him the same comfort he was offering her. The entire time he spoke, her heart was beating so fast that she was sure he could feel it. His words touched her, and she didn't like the fact that he was so hard on himself.

"You have to take the time to enjoy the little accomplishments. Otherwise, you're always striving to do better and never congratulating yourself. You can't be anything but yourself."

Daman smiled at her, and she instantly realized how contradictory that sounded.

"Funny you say that, considering you don't take your own advice."

"Yeah, I know. Guess we have a lot of work to do on ourselves."

"Guess so."

Intertwining her fingers with his, she felt like he still had something on his mind.

"What are you thinking about?"

"I was thinking about how carefree and happy you've been lately. Today, I got a chance to experience that side of you. At your grandfather's house I saw it, too, and I was hoping you would show me that side one day."

She dropped her head before meeting his gaze again. "Please don't take this personally, Daman, but sometimes with you, I purposely hold back because I don't trust you."

He tensed immediately, not liking her response.

"What I mean is that I admire your work ethic. I trust you as a partner. I trust you as a friend with benefits. But I don't trust you enough to show you all the sides of me. It's not just you. I'm like that with men in general…unless we're only friends."

"I think I deserve to know why you would trust me with your body but not all sides of your character."

His question seemed so simple, yet Imani knew the answer would sound complicated if she tried to explain. "Why does it even matter?"

"I don't know…it just does." He was disappointed, and she didn't like knowing she was the cause.

"Let's switch roles for a minute," she said, crossing one leg over the other. "There are many different sides to you, too. There's the man you want people to see and the man you really are on the inside. Do you trust me enough, Daman? Enough to show me the true you inside and out?"

At his silence, she continued.

"Did you ever think that maybe our paths were supposed to cross to allow us to believe in happily ever after? To help us realize that we can open our hearts up to that one special person fate picked out for us? If we can get this close with guarded hearts, imagine how close we could get if we opened up completely."

Daman raised an eyebrow at her statement.

"Not to each other of course, but to someone else. Maybe we met to prep each other for the real thing."

She could tell he was trying to process what she was saying. "What makes you think we couldn't have the real thing?"

She sighed. "You told me yourself that you aren't the marrying kind. And I'm not one of those women who believe they can change a man. Plus, I'm still trying my best to dig within myself to regain all those dreams I had as a girl. Yes, we lust after each other. But do us both a favor and try not to confuse this for something more than it is."

How could she tell him that he was the one man she wished she could fall for, and who she hoped would reciprocate her feelings? How could she help him understand her fear that once she opened her heart up to him, he would never fully open up to her? She knew his type, and she knew that he had commitment issues. Guarded or not, she wasn't willing to take the chance and be hurt by any man. She knew what she had to do. She would enjoy their affair for as long as it lasted.

"Can we please have this one moment without expecting anything more than what it is?" she asked in a hopeful voice.

## Chapter 16

There weren't many times when Daman didn't know what to say, but right now, he was at a loss for words. He wanted to tell Imani that he didn't think he would ever tire of wanting to taste her. He wanted to tell her that she affected him unlike any other woman in his past, and he knew he didn't deserve her. He wanted to tell her that even though she tried to act like an affair was all she wanted, he knew she wanted love, but like him, she kept her heart guarded…away from the possibility of breaking.

He couldn't say any of that, though. His fears for loving someone and losing the one he loved most in the world ran too deep. He also couldn't agree to something he knew was a lie. If his suspicions were true, then fulfilling his hunger one time would definitely not be enough—far from it. Instead, he would silently give in to her request, knowing he couldn't pass up the opportunity to be with her in the most intimate way possible.

The hand that had been resting on her leg grew increasingly bolder, as it slowly made its way up her inner thigh. With every stroke that brought his hand higher on her thigh, he felt her breath quicken. He hated that her jogging pants were in the way of his hands, gently rubbing the one fixation that kept him up at night. He wanted to savor the moment and take it slow with her. The fire in her eyes was enough to almost push him over the edge. Knowing that her desire matched his was making it harder for him to maintain his composure. He helped her up and made his way to the nearest bedroom, tugging her gently behind him.

Once in the bedroom, he turned off the light and drew her back into his arms, only to have her greet him with a soft peck before leaving his lips to plant kisses around his face, finally settling at his ears. Slowly, Imani wrapped her arms around his neck and suckled on his earlobe in the same rotation she used when they shared their first kiss. She knew the effect she had on him when she kissed his earlobes so erotically. He barely felt her lead him to the edge of the bed, until she plopped him down and straddled his body, leaving his ears to plant soft kisses along his neck.

The need to be inside her was slowly driving him mad. When Imani slightly lifted her head back toward his left ear, he took the opportunity to flip her over on her back, giving him the power to control the foreplay. The only sounds in the beach house were their moans of pleasure intertwined with the soft waves crashing against rocks.

"If I let you keep licking my neck and ears, this night won't last much longer."

"I can't help that I like the way your body reacts when I lick your neck and ears. It makes me even wetter."

Daman watched her in admiration as she pushed him off her and threw off her clothes, leaving nothing on but a lacey black panty and bra set. That classy demeanor she often maintained was gone, replaced by an uninhibited vixen. He sat in awe of every move she made, finally able to fully appreciate every curve of her delectable body.

She kneeled on the bed, seemingly overcome by the passionate aura they had created in the room. Her hair was falling freely across her shoulders, while her cat-like moves were leaving him speechless. He figured he had two options: be a bystander or be a participant.

Slowly he began to pull off her bra with his teeth, only briefly acknowledging that he was still dressed. Once her breasts were free of the material, he guided a nipple into his mouth so fast that he heard her gasp in surprise.

"Daman, please take off your clothes."

Her voice was low and breathless. He stood and threw off his clothes in record time, not wanting to be away from her for too long. But her glazed-over eyes kept his feet stationed as he let her admire his naked body.

"You're one tempting woman, Ms. Rayne."

The slight smile she gave him was soft and inviting. "And you're one sexy man, Mr. Barker. Now…are you going to keep me waiting?"

He had every intention of continuing his foreplay with her, but neither of their bodies seemed to be getting the message. Slowly, he lowered himself on top of her, gently taking her lips again. She met him halfway, slightly opening her mouth to invite him in. He'd barely kissed her, but he could feel the intense knots form throughout his entire body, brought on by their erotic intimacy. His groin was aching, and his hardness was already anticipating diving into her wet center. He placed a finger down there to see if she was ready. As soon as he reached her middle, she arched her back off the bed, not once allowing her mouth to leave his.

"Woman, you are so damn responsive! I can barely hold on any longer," Daman said between kisses.

She seductively dipped her tongue in and out of his mouth before moving to lick his ear.

"Then forget the foreplay, and bury yourself deep inside me," she whispered.

"You have such a naughty way with words. Who knew…?"

Imani giggled at his comment and released him. Within seconds, he located the condoms he'd brought, sheathed his member and lowered himself onto her again.

He opened her legs, wondering if he'd ever seen a pair of thighs that fascinated him the way Imani's did. Slowly, he eased into her center, allowing her to get used to his length. She was tight, and he knew it had been a while since she'd made love. She adjusted her body to accommodate his size, and with one final thrust, he was completely inside of her.

"You feel so good…way too good," he told her between breaths. His encouraging words caused Imani to pick up her pace, meeting him stroke for stroke. She began clenching her inner muscles in a milking effect as if she were trying to suck him in even deeper than he already was.

"What the hell is going on with you tonight?" Daman asked, more breathless than he wanted to be.

Once again, she giggled in his ear and increased her pace even more. Daman wanted this night to last for as long as it could, but the way she was moving her hips caused him to slightly lose control. Never had he felt so connected to a lover before. Her moans and soft whimpers were unnerving his body in ways he couldn't explain. He tensed up, not wanting to allow himself to feel the emotions slowly surfacing in the forefront of his mind. The concerned look on Imani's face let him know she could sense his anxiety.

"What's wrong? Are you okay?"

Daman said the first thing he could think of. "I have a cramp in my right leg. It's not a big deal. I just need to straighten my leg out a little bit."

"Oh, okay. I can fix that."

Daman let her up, assuming she was allowing him to take a quick break. Instead, she straddled him, pinned him down on the bed and lowered herself back onto the length of him. He gasped out of surprise and pleasure. He'd felt how tight she was, so he knew getting used to his size wasn't an easy task. But she'd lowered herself onto him like they'd made love a thousand times.

Imani began to rotate her hips in a circular motion, moving up and down in a rhythm that made Daman groan with pleasure. He quickly realized he couldn't control the situation. With Imani in the driver's seat, he had no choice but to let go and enjoy himself, only briefly acknowledging that he was headed in a direction he'd never gone before.

With every movement she made, her body demanded that he release himself physically and emotionally. Ever since he'd met Imani, he'd had a hard time telling his body not to react to her the way it did, and apparently, tonight was no different. He'd think about the consequences later.

Hair plastered all across her face and sweat glistening off her forehead, he knew she was close. Her thighs clinched together, forcing him to go even deeper than he already was. Two strokes later, all thoughts ceased as they both experienced an indescribable feeling of pure, unrestrained lust, releasing all their inhibitions and fears of what was yet to come.

Together, they rode out their throes of passion, as the electrifying currents tore through them. As the waves of pleasure subsided, Imani smiled that smile meant only for him and passed out on his chest in exhaustion. In that instant, as he held her, all he was thinking was that he'd never experienced anything so fulfilling in his entire life.

## Chapter 17

Slowly opening her eyes the next morning, Imani stretched out her body and felt her muscles ache in satisfaction. It had been five years since she put them to good use, and she didn't regret one thing. After four rounds of lovemaking, it was a miracle she was even up at all.

As they lay there, spooning like they had after every lovemaking session, she glanced over her shoulder at Daman and watched his eyes slowly open. Making love to him felt right, and the way they connected sexually was stronger than anything she'd ever experienced.

"I understand how you feel because I feel the same way."

All she could do was smile at Daman's response. She hadn't even said anything, yet they were so in tune with each other that he'd read the look in her eyes.

She glimpsed out of the side window at the beautiful

sunrise overlooking the calm water. "I can't believe it's morning already, can you?" she asked, as she glanced from the window up at Daman's face.

Their bodies were tangled in the sheets, and the intense look Daman was giving her made her want him all over again. They had fallen in and out of sleep throughout the night, yet she felt more relaxed than she would have if she had slept an entire eight hours.

Daman gently pushed her disarrayed hair out of her face. He wanted to go another round. She could feel it. He pulled her into him and placed a soft kiss on her lips, obviously not affected by their morning breath. She knew the type of man Daman was, but so far he had completely surprised her with how attentive he was during intimacy.

"What are you thinking?" Imani asked after he broke the kiss.

He was quiet for a second before asking her another personal question. "Why do you release a feather into the air sometimes?"

Imani sat up in bed with the sheets still wrapped around her. She knew he would want to know that eventually. "You're full of questions, aren't you?"

Daman laughed, and she thought she'd never quite heard that laugh before. It was both sexy and raspy, making him even more desirable.

"Stop stalling and answer the question."

She couldn't recall ever telling anyone besides her cousins or Mya the meaning behind releasing a feather into the air, but she wanted to tell Daman. After all, he'd caught her so many times, he deserved to know the reason.

"Gamine always loved to visit new places. She visited everyone who was important to her, and she always had a new story to tell us at the next family gathering. When she passed away, I wasn't ready to let go, even though I knew she would always be in my heart. So I decided that every time I went out of town to someplace I'd never been before, I would release a feather into the sky and hope that it reached her in heaven. That way, she always knows where I was and that I was thinking of her. I know it's silly and childish, but it helps so I shared it with a few other members having a hard time dealing with her death. And all those places she wanted to see…now she can, through us."

Daman was silent for a few seconds before responding. "I don't think it's silly or childish to do something to honor a loved one. There are things that I do to let my father know that he will never be forgotten."

Imani placed her hand on Daman's arm. "It must be hard for you to hear me talk about Gamine this way. I don't want to start thinking about your dad and make you sad after we had such a great night."

His hand grazed her cheek.

"You have nothing to be sorry about. There are times when I have entire conversations with my dad. You know, to keep him updated on my life. Some people may say that's childish and silly because he can't talk back, but I couldn't care less what they think. The only thing that matters is that I feel better talking to him."

Imani observed Daman as he continued to talk about his relationship with his father. She couldn't believe how wrong she'd been about him. He was a proud man…

that she knew. But he could also be kind and sweet. She could hear the strength in his heartfelt words.

"So do you release a feather at every new location?" Daman asked, breaking her thoughts.

"No, only the places that I would tell Gamine about if she were here. Each place where I release a feather holds a special moment, memory or person for me."

By now, Daman had moved closer to Imani and was already tugging the sheet away from her body.

"I have to admit something," Daman said in a low voice. "I've seen you release several feathers at places that I've been with you. Is it safe to say that I have something to do with a feather or two?"

There was a knock on the front door, breaking the moment between them. Daman took the extra sheet that had been dismissed to the floor and wrapped it around his waist before leaving the bedroom.

Imani was glad for the small window of alone time to process her thoughts. She realized too late that she'd mistakenly led him to believe that he could have been the reason behind the release of a couple feathers. Truth be told, she would have told Gamine about Daman if she were still alive.

*Did I subconsciously release a feather with Daman in mind?*

He returned to the bedroom with a piece of paper in his hand.

"The butler said that the Walshes will meet with us in two hours for introductions before the brunch."

"Does that mean we have time for another round?" Imani asked, trying to divert Daman from the previous topic of discussion.

"Yes, it does," Daman said in a husky voice. "But first I want to know if you have an answer for my question." He dropped the sheet and climbed back into bed.

She watched him closely as she admired his aroused state. They were both leaning on their sides and had gotten closer to one another. His face was mere inches away from hers.

"You may have had something to do with a feather, but I wouldn't get too happy about it. You're not *that* important to me," she said playfully.

"Ms. Rayne, I don't believe a word you're saying," he said, gently kissing her face. She could feel his smile between kisses.

After what they'd done last night, he didn't have any reason to believe her. She wouldn't even believe her. There was no use denying it.

"Well, Mr. Barker, when you're right, you're right."

She didn't understand this submissive side of herself, but she didn't want to focus on it now. She would worry about her feelings later. For now, she wanted to direct all of her attention toward the man who was making her lose her self-control.

When his hands were on her body, it made her feel alive. Every touch left a heated mark in its trail, and under his intense gaze and steamy kisses, she lost herself in their passion.

"You have no idea how beautiful you are."

She looked into his eyes and saw the appreciation reflected in them. "When you stare at me the way you do, it's hard not to feel beautiful."

Leaning down, she kissed him with all the emotion that had been buried inside her for years. She always knew she was attractive, but Daman looked at her in a way that made her feel like he only had eyes for her. She knew that wasn't possible, since he'd made sure she understood that he loved women and had no intentions to commit to only one.

Imani willed her thoughts to cease so that she could focus on the desire building inside of her. He put on a condom, and slowly, she eased him inside of her and began rocking her hips to the tranquil sounds of the water. Inch by glorious inch, he filled her. She clenched and unclenched when she rocked on his member. Daman rewarded her with groans of pleasure.

The faster she rode, the louder their moans grew, mixing with the soft squeak of the bed. Daman grabbed her butt and lifted his knees, matching her movements in a rhythm created just for them. She knew Daman felt the exact moment he hit her sweet spot. The magnitude of pleasure she felt almost had her bucking off the bed, but Daman tightened his grip…refusing to let her go.

She looked into his eyes, determined to plea for him to release her a little, but the eyes that stared back at her displayed no signs of remorse. He seemed ready for a strong orgasm and began to match her movements harder and faster. Her mind and heart told her to shut him out and control the situation. But when he smirked at her, fire burning in his eyes, her body refused to listen to her mind or her heart. Instead, she chose to give in to temptation and tighten her inner walls around him.

The movement caught him off guard because seconds later he threw back his head and grunted her name in an unrecognizable voice. Together they soared over mountains and valleys as they were hit with orgasms so strong, they felt like they were neither here nor there, but in a place all their own.

As Imani sat on a chair wearing Daman's discarded T-shirt, she marveled at the beautiful Sunday sunrise. Brunch with the Walshes yesterday had been successful, and she eagerly texted Vicky that the Walshes agreed to sponsor two events for this year's pre-gala parties.

Taking a sip of her coffee, she glanced over at Daman still asleep in bed. Even though the sheet was covering his body, she still admired the shape of his strong thighs and tight butt. That man had no right to look that damn fine. He was definitely a sight she could get accustomed to seeing every day, which triggered that voice inside her head warning her that she was in danger of falling even harder. She'd hoped to remain sleeping with him in bed until they caught a flight back later that day. But she wasn't so lucky.

She'd been receiving texts and calls all morning and was trying her best to keep her emotions at bay. Today was her grandmother's birthday and undoubtedly one of the hardest days for her every year. She'd been so focused on not falling for Daman, that she'd forgotten how monumental the day was for the Burrstones.

Her family always turned to her for comfort, oblivious of the fact that there were some days she'd rather be the one receiving the comfort. She missed everything about Gamine and it was days like today that took her back to that sad and tragic day five years ago when she found out that the one person she'd loved most in the world, was no longer physically here.

The morning Gamine passed away, Imani had known something was wrong. She felt it in the chilly April air around her and her day seemed to move in slow motion.

The moment she'd walked through the front door of the Burrstone home, she could hear the heart-wrenching sobs and quiet whispers of neighbors and close friends echoing through the large household. Her immediate family was nowhere in sight, and everyone that she passed refused to make eye contact with her.

As she'd rounded the doorway leading to the dining room, her mother was the first person she saw. Hope was hunched in a chair, crying uncontrollably, while Imani's father and Cyd stood close behind. Imani immediately went to her mother and cradled her pained face in her hands. The redness of her mother's hazel eyes disguised their true beauty as they tenderly stared into Imani's face. She had never seen her mother look so upset and her mother's words that day would forever be imprinted in her mind.

"She's gone, Imani. My heart is breaking because no one can bring my mother back to me. I didn't even get a chance to say goodbye. Why her?" her mother had shrieked as she looked up toward the ceiling. "Dear God, why her?" Imani's aunts had rushed to her mother's side, cradling her in their arms, as they cried together for the loss of their mother. Hope may have been her mother's name, but Imani had never seen her look so hopeless.

Imani's thoughts were broken when she heard the ruffling of the sheet. She glanced over at Daman again, but this time he was staring right at her. He tilted his head to the side, studying the stressed features on her face. She saw the question in his eyes and realized that he probably noticed the tension in her eyes caused by unshed tears. She momentarily forgot about the importance of the day as she watched him walk toward her in all his naked glory.

"Is everything okay?" Daman asked, placing her coffee on the table while lifting her from the chair. Once they reached the bed, he laid down and motioned for her to lie down, too.

"I'm fine," Imani lied. "I just couldn't sleep."

Daman looked at her questionably, not believing her answer. "I heard your phone ring and vibrate a few times. Are you sure everything's okay?" Stroking her cheek, he gazed into her eyes, continuing to comfort her without words.

"You're right, I'm not fine," Imani replied after a few minutes of silence. "Today is Gamine's birthday."

Daman's eyes squinted together in understanding. "I see…" As he pulled her closer to him, Imani leaned into his chest relishing in his comforting touch.

"I've tried for years to forget that day, yet on Gamine's birthday every year, my family calls on me for support and just when I think I'll be able to get through the day without having my own emotional breakdown, my emotions fail me."

She shivered at the possibility of that happening again and pulled the sheet over her body to slow down her quivering.

"Do you want to talk more about that day?" Daman asked. "You talked about Gamine and your responsibilities a little on Friday, but I have a feeling you haven't really talked to many people about it. It may help you deal with pain if you talk about it."

Imani didn't dare tell him that he was right and that she hadn't really talked to anyone about that day. Maybe opening up would help her deal with the emotions battling inside her.

"The day she passed away, all I wanted to do was cry until I had no tears left and scream until I had no words left to speak. But I couldn't do that. Gamine had groomed me, telling me that I was the nurturer among the grandchildren and that I would eventually have to step up in the family when no one else could."

Daman began gliding his hand up and down her arm. "That's a lot of pressure to place on someone."

Imani nodded her head. "It was...it definitely was. And I hadn't truly known what Gamine meant until that day. It's easy to tell someone you understand, but it's much harder to realize the true meaning behind the lesson until it hits you full force."

"I couldn't agree more," Daman added.

When he didn't continue, Imani realized that he wanted to give her a chance to continue speaking. But she wanted to learn more about Daman.

"Did your father make you feel the same way?"

"More or less. My father was a very determined man, and my mother is always very supportive. At a young age, they provided me with the tools they believed I would need to succeed. My father was big on integrity, and he made sure I realized that success has to be earned. No one will hand you your dreams on a silver platter, and throughout his journey for success, he never stepped on anyone's toes to achieve his dreams.

He always kept his integrity and never once changed his character to satisfy another individual." Daman's voice tensed slightly as if reflecting on a bad memory.

Imani caught the edge in his voice.

"What's wrong?"

After a few minutes, Imani wondered if Daman would answer her question. When he began speaking, his comforting eyes grew distant and serious.

"I remember being in the hospital after my father's car crash, listening to the doctors tell my mother and me that they couldn't stop the internal bleeding. I didn't even stay in the hallway long enough to listen to the doctor explain how many hours we had left with him. There were a lot of things rushing through my mind that day, but the one that hit me the hardest was the fact that I'd just received my undergraduate degree and it was a day before my father would make me a permanent full-time employee at Barker Architecture. I'd worked there since I was sixteen so I knew the company better than most of the employees. Officially becoming a member of the executive team at such a young age was an honor and an experience I was excited to share with my father."

As Imani listened to Daman talk, she couldn't recall ever hearing a story that related to hers so closely. Both had lost a loved one earlier than expected and by the tone in Daman's voice, he was still dealing with the loss like she was.

"My mother couldn't even bear to tell my father right away so when we walked into his hospital room, she just broke down and cried. I watched my father gather all his strength to console her in a tight hug. As I looked into his eyes, I could tell he knew he didn't have much longer. The crazy thing is, I didn't even cry that day. I felt like I had to cry, but not one tear came out. It was almost as if I was watching someone else's life and not my own."

"I know the feeling," Imani added as she twirled her hand in soft circles on his shoulder.

Daman pulled her even closer to the fit of him. "How did Gamine pass away again?"

Imani sighed. "She passed away in her sleep. We aren't sure what caused her death. During that time, the family members who wanted to know what caused her death outweighed the family members that didn't."

"That's terrible," Daman replied. "Not knowing what caused her death. Do you feel like you're missing a piece of an unsolved puzzle?"

It baffled Imani how close Daman was to the truth. "All the time," Imani answered. "Gamine and I were extremely close, but the day she died there was no time to dwell on my pain or ask God why it happened. My family was enduring a lot of anguish, and the initial shock was still present on each of their faces. I needed to remain strong that day and questioning grieving relatives who didn't want an autopsy wasn't an option I entertained. My parents were against it, as well, which made the decision even harder to accept. Gamine was my mother's world, and it pained me to see her taking Gamine's death so much harder than any of her siblings."

Her voice staggered as she thought about her mom and other relatives on the day Gamine passed away.

Her father's disposition still disheartened her when she thought about him that day.

"My father was the first person to tell me the news. I remember him constantly rubbing a hand across the back of his neck, as if he were straining to find the right words. He was shaking his head and exhaling, the tension emanating from his body. My father always knew what to say, but during that moment, he clearly strained to find the right words. Just like your mom was with your dad."

Daman only offered a small smile, but his eyes reflected understanding.

"My sister didn't say much that day. We embraced and she cried softly on my shoulder, but like I said the other day, she was pretty withdrawn. The only statement she said to me was to look at my grandfather. One look at the man and I'd known why my sister had prompted me to pay attention. We knew my grandfather was devastated, yet his pain was hidden behind a stoic mask. He's always been a man of few words so he remained silent most of the day. But those who knew him well could see the agony, distress and disbelief behind the mask. For him, the sun rose and set in Gamine. That day, we all grieved for a mother, a grandmother and a friend, but my grandfather lost the love of his life."

Although his face remained normal, Imani felt Daman tense and she took note that he'd stopped rubbing her arm, and instead clenched the sheet into his fist. On instinct, Imani placed her hand over his clenched fist and began massaging out the tension until he released the sheet. She watched him look down at his hand, then back up at her face. She didn't know what was wrong or how she'd triggered that emotion from him, but she wanted to put him back at ease.

She pulled his face closer to hers and placed a soft kiss on his lips. He returned her kiss and pulled her even closer to him.

"Thanks," Daman said after the kiss ended. "I needed that."

"Is everything okay?" Imani asked, observing the lines of stress that were creased in his forehead.

He looked into her eyes and sighed. "When my dad passed away, I grew extremely close to my uncle Frank. He's the president of Barker Architecture, and he took me under his wing, treating me like the son he never had."

Daman paused and ran his hand down his face. "Recently, I've learned that he's not the man I thought he was and may be a threat to Barker Architecture. It feels like I lost another person I love. Another mentor and father figure."

He stopped talking again and looked Imani straight in the eyes. "Physically, I lost a father. Mentally, I lost my mom for a while over the devastation of losing my father. And now, I've lost my uncle. It seems the people I tend to love most are the ones I lose first."

Imani knew it was hard for Daman to open up so she was glad he was expressing himself to her. She was curious about his uncle, but she didn't want to push the subject. *Is he trying to warn me that he will never care for a woman that deeply?*

She was pretty sure he was doing just that. "I understand," Imani said, rubbing her hand on his cheek, wanting to bring him comfort.

"There are two things my dad told me when he was dying," Daman said after a few minutes of silence. "He wanted me to take care of Barker Architecture by continuing to make the company prosperous. I've been working toward that since he passed away, but this year I've really invested more time into figuring out every past and present detail about the company."

"What was the second thing?" Imani asked when he didn't continue. His eyes softened a little before he answered.

"The second thing he asked me to do was purchase the estate on the lake." Imani's heart dropped at the mention of the estate. "He didn't tell me why, but he also knew he didn't need to. There was no way I wasn't fulfilling his wish. That still stands true."

She debated with the idea of telling Daman her reason for wanting the estate and decided she could be truthful as well.

"A few months before Gamine passed away she was bugging me every week about the estate with the lake view that was owned by Mr. and Mrs. Sims. She told me the estate was perfect for me and would hold all the answers I'd been searching for. I never really paid it any attention until she passed away, and suddenly I felt more lost than I ever had in my entire life."

She thought she would see surprise on Daman's face, but instead she saw understanding. She snuggled into his arms and rested her head under his chin. Both of them wanted the estate and neither knew what they were actually searching for. But she wouldn't give up, and she was pretty sure Daman wouldn't, either.

As she lay in the arms of the only person standing in

the way of her owning the estate, she reflected on the past few years of her life. Talking to Daman made her face issues within herself that she'd been struggling to pinpoint for years. In the process of her trying to fill Gamine's shoes, she'd lost sight of who she was as a woman. She'd lost touch of her sensuality and her desire to belong to one man for the rest of her life. She'd become consumed with her idea of being the ideal family member and friend, not once taking the time for herself.

She'd placed her life on hold the day Gamine passed away, and the only solution she knew would work was purchasing the estate and seeing if it brought her the closure she needed.

"I wonder if there is anyone else in the world who remembers the exact moment their life stood still," Imani said aloud. "I remember my moment to the second." She sat upright in the bed and crossed her legs, facing Daman. "The day we lost Gamine, after I consoled my family members and friends, I sat on a chair in the corner of my grandfather's home and counted to ten several times. My body felt weightless, my heart ached beyond measure and my mind was racing with the fear of what was to come. I grew numb, not believing that without warning my life had changed in an instant."

She glanced out the window and then back at Daman. "Don't you think it's unusual that a moment so sad and tragic has defined my life so far more than any accomplishments I've made?"

Daman leaned up in bed on one elbow. "It may not be normal, but now that you've heard my story, you know there's at least one other person who understands exactly how you feel." With that, he pulled her onto him for another sweet and tender kiss.

## Chapter 18

The Burrstone barbecue was in full swing and Imani was a nervous wreck. She had successfully avoided Daman since their rendezvous in St. Simons Island. She thought not seeing him for a couple weeks would be enough time to steer her back into reality, but today she wasn't so sure.

Daman had invited her to go with him to Atlanta to check on things, but she lied and told him she was too busy at work. Truthfully, she wasn't busy at all, but the less they saw of each other, the better. She still hadn't quite gotten hold of her emotions.

Her pink maxi dress swayed slightly in the wind as she walked into her grandfather's huge backyard. She quickly scanned the attendees to make sure Daman hadn't arrived yet. Confirming that he hadn't, she was able to admire the great job she and her cousins had done planning the barbecue. The grandchildren were really starting to step it up in her family, and she was proud of all of them.

"Hey, Imani. Is your man here yet?"

Imani turned her head and rolled her eyes, but Cyd seemed indifferent and unfazed by the look.

"Seriously, Cyd, would it kill you and everyone else to stop with the teasing and leave well enough alone? He is not my man. We're just…"

"Business partners. I know, I know. Please don't tell me for the hundredth time. You've got to lighten up because it's not that serious. How many times do I need to tell you that?"

Cyd smiled at Imani as she gave her a quick hug.

Imani sighed and returned her smile. "You're right. I'm overreacting."

She returned Cyd's hug, and the two continued into the house to meet with the female family and friends who usually gathered in the beautiful sunroom Gamine had created. Her grandmother always felt like the den was the men's domain and that the women of the family and neighborhood should have their own domain, as well.

"Have you seen Mom and Dad yet?"

"Nope. But Mom texted me that they were on their way. And I should warn you that Mom and the aunts are already betting on how long it will take you and Daman to admit your feelings for one another. Everyone is ready for a wedding. They hate the fact that everyone in our generation is single."

Imani creased her eyes together as she felt her irritation return. "Please tell me you're joking."

"Nope. Dead serious," Cyd said with a giggle. "But don't forget that you just said it wasn't a big deal."

"Sis, for real, how well do you know me?"

"Extremely well," she said with a laugh.

"How well do you know our family?"

"Even better," Cyd answered with another laugh, understanding where the conversation was headed.

"Then you already know why I'm nervous."

"Nervous about what?" Mya asked.

Imani and Cyd turned around to find Mya and Lex walking toward them. The house was quickly filling with people, so instead of answering Mya's question, Imani headed to the backyard, knowing the ladies would follow her. Unfortunately, that didn't stop Mya from repeating her question as they made their way through the house.

"As if you don't know. I'm nervous about if the family will make this day a very big deal for Daman and me. The Burrstones are a lot to handle, and we aren't even dating." She was speaking quietly, trying to refrain from being overheard by people passing by them.

"You're right, I did know. I just wanted to hear you say it," Mya said with a sarcastic laugh. "You need to stop trippin' and get over it. Maybe if the two of you hadn't broadcasted your relationship on national radio, you wouldn't be going through this now."

"I could blame *you* all for that. And we didn't broadcast anything because nothing is or was going on with us. Everyone just heard what they wanted to hear."

"You're right, Imani. Everyone imagined that there was something going on between you and Daman. Everyone is wrong, and you're right."

Imani gave Mya a stern look similar to the one she'd given Cyd countless times. And like Cyd, Mya seemed unfazed by it.

"This hot and cold thing with you has got to stop, girl. Quit fighting how you feel about him."

"You know what? As much as I love your honesty sometimes, today you're really aggravating me."

Mya nonchalantly shrugged her shoulders.

"That goes for you, too, Cyd."

Cyd held up her hands in defeat. "Don't bring me into it. I stopped talking about it."

"Ah, Imani. Mya and I were actually looking for you to tell you…"

"Oh, no Lex, not you, too. I think I've heard enough from these two," Imani said, pointing at Cyd and Mya.

"But what if I know you want to hear what I have to say?" Lex asked in a sugary voice, insinuating that she knew a secret.

Imani didn't like the exchange of looks between Mya and Cyd and decided if they knew what Lex had to say, then she had better listen. Lex hadn't said much as she laughed at the charade between Imani and Mya, so she knew it could be important.

"Okay, but let's get out of this house because the aunts are starting to stare at me, and Mom will join them any minute when she gets here."

"Are you sure you'd rather not stay here?" Lex asked.

"No, not at all! I've been trying to make my way out of this house for the last ten minutes."

"Hmm…well, okay then. Let's go."

The four women made their way out of the house to the backyard, and Imani immediately stopped dead in her tracks. She couldn't see Daman, but she could feel his presence. It felt like time stood still as she glanced around the backyard, finally spotting him standing at a picnic table with Jaleen and Taheim. He looked every bit of sexy in his jeans and blue button-up. He hadn't spotted her yet, which was great because her mouth was already dry just looking at him. She didn't need to be paralyzed by the dark embers in his eyes, too.

As if on cue, he scanned the backyard until he landed right on Imani. She sucked in a much-needed breath at the intensity of his stare.

"Girl, I almost told you he was out here, but I'm so glad you didn't let me," Lex said with an appreciative smile. "I think we already suspected how much you affect him, but that look from him confirms it. Daman's looking at you like you'll be his dessert for the day."

"Yeah, the chemistry is pretty obvious," Cyd chimed in. "No matter how much you try to hide it."

Mya shook her head as she looked at her best friend and business partner.

"See, at first I was going to ask you if anything had happened between you and Daman when you were in St. Simons Island. But knowing what a closet freak you are, I'm pretty sure we can all guess what happened."

That comment was enough to break the exchange between Imani and Daman, as she turned toward the women.

"Don't look at me like that. You know I'm telling the truth."

"Mya's right, Imani," Lex commented. "We knew sooner or later Daman would break you out of that shell you've developed. Playing hard to get is one thing, but acting like you aren't interested is another. Who are you trying to fool? Him, us or yourself?"

They were right, and quite frankly, she was tired of fighting it. She really was jumping back and forth with her feelings for Daman, and it wasn't like her to be so indecisive. Gamine's death had really changed her, and in some cases, not for the better.

"Okay, here's the thing. Yes, something did happen between us. Yes, I'm confused about my feelings. And yes, everyone does have a reason to believe we are more than business partners."

She momentarily looked back over her shoulder at Daman and found him still staring at her. "And ladies, that man worked me more than any other man I've ever met."

"Now that's more like the sister I know."

She glanced at the women again. "Okay, so now y'all know what happened. What should I do?"

"Well first, I think you need to loosen up," Lex replied. "You're both adults, and what you do behind closed doors is your business. I don't see anything wrong with spending time with him."

"And enjoying other things about him," Cyd interjected. "You're thinking about it too hard, Imani."

She stole another glance at Daman and was glad to see he wasn't staring at her anymore. Gamine always told her that everything happened for a reason, and right now, there had to be a reason she'd met Daman. She knew making a move at her family's barbecue would be making a big statement because a lot of eyes were on her. But she also knew that the old her didn't always care, so the new her had to learn not to, as well.

"Ladies, I think you're right. No more treating my feelings like a Ping-Pong ball. From now on, all bets are off. As good as that sex was, I need to get sixths and sevenths. All work and no play is not a good combination."

Even though she'd said it before, this time she meant it. Somehow Daman was slowly helping her become her old self again, and it was about time that she learned to accept it.

"Wait a minute, sixths and sevenths?" Cyd asked. "Umm, does Daman have a brother?"

"Or a cousin?" Lex added with a laugh.

Mya reached over and placed her arm around Imani's shoulder.

"Welcome back, kid," she said teasingly. "Now, go greet your man."

Cyd and Lex laughed, nodding their heads in agreement.

As Imani made her way to Daman, her heart was racing. She didn't dare look around the backyard for fear all eyes were on her.

"You'd think they all had nothing better to do," Imani mumbled to herself.

Years ago, her generation had learned not to bring dates to family functions because the Burrstone clan would definitely make the couple the center of attention. Apparently, that fact was still true.

As she reached the group of men, she hugged Taheim and Jaleen and stopped in front of Daman. She didn't know if she should risk hugging him, too, but she didn't want to be rude by hugging his friends and not him. So she leaned slightly into Daman, and he instantly took control of the hug. He buried his face in the crease of her neck and softly whispered that she was beautiful. The spark was instant, and she couldn't control the electric current that shot through her body. When she leaned away from him to look into his face, his eyes dropped down to her lips again. His arms tensed under her touch, indicating that he was trying to control the urge to kiss her. Even so, she still felt their faces getting closer and closer to each other.

"Imani, you didn't hug me like that," Taheim said with a laugh. "I feel left out."

Imani softly punched Taheim in the arm but was happy for the interruption. The looks on Jaleen's and Taheim's faces proved they knew that Daman had come close to kissing her in front of her family and friends.

"I missed you," Daman said, obviously not caring that his friends could hear him. She was surprised he made that declaration, and it made her want to kiss him even more.

"Do you want to go somewhere and talk?" she asked him.

"Yeah, let's go." Daman gave a head nod to Taheim and Jaleen as Imani gently took his hand. She went past the crowd of guests in the backyard and led Daman down a walking path outlined by weeping willow trees until they arrived at a cozy pond surrounded by beautiful greenery.

Imani led him to a rock formation with a small waterfall seeping through the rocks. The formation was almost completely hidden in the beautiful landscape making this area of the huge backyard a very private place.

"Wow," was the only word that escaped Daman's lips.

"My grandfather built this area for my grandmother because she loved being in her own backyard. We call this area Gamine's Haven."

When they reached a small seeped-in section of the rock formation, Imani looked into Daman's eyes. They had so much to talk about, but she wasn't in the mood for talking. As if reading her thoughts, Daman slowly walked backward until he felt his back hit the smooth part of a large rock. He grabbed Imani's arm and pulled her to him.

"I missed you, too," Imani said, as she leaned in to kiss him.

Words weren't necessary, as her tongue found his, and she slowly began suckling on the tip, reconfirming the honeyed taste she'd missed. He smelled all male in that make-you-want-to-drop-your-panties kind of way. Imani didn't understand how she'd gone her entire life without being kissed like Daman kissed her.

Daman's hands slowly made their way to her butt, grabbing it and pulling her closer to the fit of his inner thighs. She could hear the chatter in the backyard and the sound of kids playing in the distance, but she blocked out all of the noise as she focused solely on the way Daman was making her feel.

His hands briefly left her butt to immerse themselves in her hair. The butterflies in her stomach grew bigger and bigger as they continued their exotic foreplay. She felt Daman slowly lift up her dress. She hadn't known how high he'd lifted it until she felt two of his fingers dip inside her panties and into her moist center. She couldn't hold the gasp that escaped her throat as he began to twirl his fingers, quickly plunging them in and out. He'd found her G-spot, and he planned to work her right there, in broad daylight. His kisses grew more passionate, and she felt the orgasm inside of her threaten to break free.

"Daman, if you don't slow down, I'm going to have an orgasm," she said breathlessly in his ear.

"Then I guess you better prepare yourself because there's no way I'm slowing down."

With that said, Daman further increased the tempo of his fingers, releasing the orgasm that Imani had tried to hold back. She screamed in his mouth as she leaned into him for support, her legs growing weak from the intensity. When Daman dropped her dress back down, all she could think about doing was giving him the same release.

Unzipping his pants and looking down at his member, she wondered how he would taste. She'd never gone down on a man before and swore she'd never do such a thing. But for some reason, she wanted to please him in a different way and knew the action would probably shock him.

Squatting down and adjusting her body in the small space, she secretly thanked her yoga instructor for increasing her flexibility. She looked up at Daman and could tell he was wondering exactly what she would do. She leaned closer to him and closed her mouth around his shaft, loving the way his body jerked from the contact. Slowly, she began licking him from top to bottom, hearing his growls increase as her hands went to work. He grew even harder in her mouth, and she loved the solid feel of him. Daman tried to say something to her, but his speech was broken. Imani didn't mind not knowing what he'd tried to say. She took the opportunity to rotate her tongue in an even quicker up and down motion. Minutes later he was on the brink, and she knew it. With one last lick, he released himself into her mouth. She suckled him dry, thinking he tasted exactly how she thought he would…sweet and tangy all mixed together.

She stood up and smoothed out Daman's wrinkled shirt while he zipped his jeans. They were both still breathing heavily from their oral foreplay. She was glad she kept extra toiletries at her grandfather's house so she could clean herself up a bit. After smoothing out her dress and her hair, she leaned into him and stared into his eyes. She could get lost in those eyes all day, and they spoke to her in ways she knew his voice never could. Still, she couldn't ignore the voice in her head that told her to be careful of this man. He was everything she'd ever wanted in a companion, but she couldn't let her heart confuse love with lust. Kissing him was the only time she felt like they were on the same page, so she did what she enjoyed doing most with him…she kissed him.

Seconds later, Daman took control of the kiss, making love to her tongue as he had her body weeks before. Imani could usually multitask, but when Daman seductively kissed her, all she could do was focus on the kiss. She failed to hear the branches crunching under footsteps that were getting closer to Gamine's Haven.

"Daman, it's so nice to see you again. I see you and my daughter are getting better acquainted," Mrs. Rayne said with a smile.

Hearing her mom's voice instantly made her stop kissing Daman. They both turned around to see her parents standing nearby. She could tell Daman was embarrassed, and so was she. She couldn't recall her parents ever catching her in such a compromising position. Mrs. Rayne was smiling, but Mr. Rayne was not.

Imani was trying to figure out what to say, but it was her father who decided to speak next.

"Daman, do you think you can stop groping my daughter long enough for me to have a quick chat with you?"

"Yes, Mr. Rayne," Daman said, as he let out a nervous laugh.

Her father walked over and roughly gripped Daman's shoulders. Imani thought her usually upbeat dad was uncomfortable after catching her and Daman, until he winked at her and kissed her forehead.

"Don't worry, baby. I won't be too hard on my future son-in-law."

Imani was embarrassed by his comment, but at least he was joking and wasn't upset.

"Dad, please don't say that."

Mr. Rayne laughed and led Daman away from Gamine's Haven. Imani turned toward her mom, who still had a smile on her face.

"Mom, stop smiling at me like that. It wasn't what it looked like."

Mrs. Rayne walked over to Imani and gently brushed some fallen hair out of her face.

"Imani, if you feel something for Daman, don't run away from it. You never were a runner, and I definitely don't want you putting on your running shoes now."

She knew exactly what her mom meant and wasn't surprised that she knew Imani was ready to run from the possibility of falling for Daman.

"I know, Mom, but what Daman and I have is just for fun. We're working on developing a friendship, but nothing more. I know you, Dad and the family are waiting for all of us young people to get married, and being your oldest child, I know you want me to settle down first. But Daman isn't the relationship type, and that suits me just fine because I don't want a relationship, anyway."

"Oh, baby. For someone so smart, you can be so dense sometimes. If you think the way Daman looks at you is how a business partner looks at another partner, then you are sadly mistaken. That man is taken with you, and it's obvious to anyone around you that it's more than a partnership. And I don't recall you having many friends who you kiss like you just kissed Daman."

She blushed. "It was just a kiss, Mom, nothing more."

"It was more than a kiss, and I wasn't born yesterday. I can tell you two have moved beyond kissing, but if you're in denial, then I won't sit here and try to convince you."

Imani looked into her mother's eyes and was glad to see happiness in them. It had been a while since she'd seen that gleam that she had when Gamine was alive.

"Imani, can you promise me one thing?"

"Sure, Mom, what is it?"

She noticed her mother's eyes were watery and she felt her mother's hand gently massaging the back of her head.

"Promise me that no matter what happens with Daman, you will continue down the path you are on now. You seem happy…really happy. For a while I felt guilty for not being there for you when Gamine passed away and forcing you into a role that no one else in the family could handle at the time. You looked after so many people, and still do. And I feel like you lost yourself along the way. Baby, you finally seem like you're breaking down a little of that hard shell you developed around your heart because you felt like you had to worry about me and the rest of the family."

Imani couldn't stop the tears that ran down her face. For so long, she felt like the family would never get back to normal, and it seemed that the person she was worried about the most was finally healing from the loss of Gamine.

"Imani, baby, I'm fine…I am fine. We're all fine, and I think it's time for you to stop devoting all your time to being there for us and finally take the time to do something for yourself."

Imani wiped the tears from her face. "Thanks for telling me that, Mom. I don't want you to feel guilty because I'd be there for you again in a heartbeat. I know a part of us left when Gamine passed away, but you're my mom, so you were always my main concern. I'm so glad to see you happy again. I really missed you, Mom."

Mrs. Rayne wiped the tears from her own face and hugged Imani with all the love she had in her heart. "I missed you, too, baby…I missed you, too. Now enough of this crying," Mrs. Rayne said, as she continued to wipe her tears. "Let's go back to the barbecue. Cyd told me you and Daman were walking down the path, but I didn't think we'd catch you two kissing. For future reference, I think you need to find a better hiding spot."

Imani laughed at her mom's suggestion. She was right. There was no telling who else might have seen them had her parents not made their presence known. She was even more anxious about the fact that her parents could have caught them earlier, which would have been way more embarrassing. She'd never done anything so daring surrounded by people, let alone family and friends. Even so, she'd enjoyed every minute of their risky foreplay. Reminiscing about how carried away they'd gotten, she wondered how many more secret public places they could find to please one another.

Instead of walking to the backyard where the barbecue was still going on, Daman decided he needed to take a quick walk. He hadn't seen Imani since her parents showed up to the barbecue. It was dark outside now, and he loved the fact that he could see the stars in this part of Illinois. Gazing up at the stars was always something he used to do with his dad. They would lie on the grass, and he'd tell Daman stories about his childhood. Stan Barker was a man who enjoyed the simple things in life, and Daman couldn't recall the exact moment he stopped remembering the values his father continually instilled in him when he was young.

When he lost his father, he swore that, with the exception of his mom, he would never let anyone get that close to him because the pain of losing someone you loved was a pain he couldn't bear to go through again. All these years, he'd not let a woman get close because he used the excuse that he was more focused on his career than building a relationship. But he was lying to himself. He knew the famous Tennyson quote, "Tis better to have loved and lost than never to have loved at all" wasn't true. For him, it was better to never love than to love and lose that person. His mind drifted back to Imani. Mr. Rayne was a good man, and Daman already admired him, even though they'd only shared a couple of conversations. Mr. Rayne's words still echoed in his mind:

*Daman, you seem like an honorable man with a good head on your shoulders, and I can tell that you come from a supportive family. You're a true career man with an admirable reputation, and that's something to be very proud of. You see, my daughter is a career woman. Strong. Determined. Her mother and I raised both our daughters with strong family values and the idea that they can accomplish anything they want in life. We are beyond proud of what they've accomplished. But don't let Imani's exterior fool you, because inside that career-driven woman is a girl who, more than anything, wants a family like the one she was raised in. With Imani, family comes first, and everything else comes second. If you are the man my daughter chooses, I'm pleased for you both because I know you can make each other very happy. But if you don't think you can be the man she needs, then you should move out of the way and make room for a man that can. I think I know how you feel, but I'll let you figure that out on your own.*

Daman wished he knew how Mr. Rayne thought he felt, because right now, he was confused. He liked the Burrstone clan, but he'd mainly wanted to go to the barbecue to see Imani. Anytime he wasn't around her, the only thing he could think about was when he was going to see her again. They'd barely gotten a chance to talk today, but what they had done said more to him than words probably could have. He couldn't recall ever lusting after a woman so much. The way she'd gone down on him had completely caught him off guard. She did it with ease and grace, which made him laugh, since those were not two words you thought about when referring to oral sex.

With Imani, he was quickly learning that she wasn't your ordinary woman. When she looked into his eyes, he felt like they were communicating without words. She noticed things about him that the majority of people in his life never noticed. The idea of another man getting to be with her angered him more than he wished it did. He had to figure out what to do, and he had to figure it out fast because the only thing he was certain about was that walking away from Imani was not an option.

Walking back to the house, he ignored that inner voice that told him he was falling for her. When he reached the backyard, he noticed most of the people he knew weren't out there. A glance into the family-room window proved they'd gone inside. Instantly, his eyes landed on Imani as she laughed at something her sister had said. She'd pulled her hair up into a ponytail, so he could see every part of her face now. What was it about her that made him forget why he'd steered clear of women like her all these years?

He stepped through the sliding door and into the living room. People were talking and laughing all around him, but his eyes stayed on Imani as he made his way to where his friends and she stood. She finally looked up at him, and he instantly felt a kick in his gut. It was a feeling he'd grown accustomed to since meeting her. They weren't even standing close, but the distance wasn't enough to get rid of the sexual tension he felt emanating between their bodies. If their friends noticed it, they weren't letting on. He wanted to finish what they'd started earlier that day. Her eyes promised that in due time, they would.

## Chapter 19

Jogging on her treadmill did nothing to clear Imani's mind. Daman was headed over to pick her up so they could discuss the final details of the gala before they headed to Atlanta, and all she could think about was how soon they could wrap up their meeting so that they could finish what they'd started at the barbecue last week. The only thing her jog had managed to do was sweat out her hair a little. She hoped her shower would do the trick, instead.

She and Daman had seen each other several times since the barbecue, but each time had been a short lunch meeting or afternoon coffee. They both had gone to Atlanta once in the past couple weeks, but were there at separate times. It had actually felt strange being in Atlanta without Daman.

Tonight, they were going on their first real date. She

knew it seemed backward, considering they'd already done plenty of naughty things that should be done after you've dated someone for a while, but she didn't care. The game she was playing with Daman was a dangerous one, but she planned to enjoy every minute of it until it was time for them to part ways.

She heard a knock at her door and wished she hadn't told the doorman she was expecting Daman. Because he had sent Daman right up without announcing him, she didn't get the chance to take that final look at her hair and outfit.

Opening the door for Daman, her breath caught in her throat. He looked extremely sexy in his blazer, shirt and pants. She'd seen him dressed nicely plenty of times, but the way he looked in this outfit was stimulating her insides more than usual. Tonight he looked extra tasty, and she didn't have the willpower to keep her hands to herself.

Gracefully, she touched the inner lining of his blazer, instantly wishing she could strip him of the material that kept her from seeing his muscles through his shirt. She heard him take a deep breath and looked up to find him observing her from head to toe. His look of approval told her he appreciated the way her black dress softly clung to her hips, accentuating her figure. She turned slightly to the right to give him a good view of her backside. Hearing another intake of breath made her laugh.

"Come here," Daman said, pulling her to him.

Her laughing ceased as he dropped his head to hers to steal a kiss. The simple kiss quickly turned lethal, as did every kiss she shared with Daman. She couldn't recall when kissing him had become so natural. If she were honest with herself, she knew it had been like that from the very first kiss they shared. She welcomed the butterflies in her stomach that grew more plentiful as his hands dropped to her butt, pulling her closer to his center. He ended the kiss when breathing became a difficult task.

"You look beautiful. Are you ready to go?"

"Yes, and you don't look too bad yourself."

Tossing her purse over her shoulder, she locked her door and linked arms with Daman. They were headed to Michael Jordan's new restaurant downtown, and Imani couldn't wait to check it out.

When they arrived at the restaurant, they were immediately seated in a private corner. She didn't want to waste any time. The quicker they got down to business, the quicker they could get on with their date.

"Can you believe the gala is approaching so soon?"

Daman shook his head and smiled. "Not really. It seems like just yesterday the Simses were asking us to host and plan the event. Did you ever wonder why they didn't ask you and your partners to plan the gala? After all, it is what you do."

Imani had actually thought about it several times, but she didn't know why they hadn't asked. "I don't know, but my partners didn't seem to mind, so I didn't, either. Besides, we're extremely busy right now, and since I'm helping with the plans, the girls have been even busier."

She didn't want to bring up the estate, but she figured Daman probably always kept the competition in perspective, so she should, too.

"Maybe it's not really up to us to choose who gets the estate after all, and they will decide after seeing how we handled the gala."

She noticed Daman clench his jaw before slightly smiling.

"Maybe," he responded.

He leaned over the table and grabbed her resting hand. She wondered what he was thinking and wished she had the courage to ask him. Instead, she decided to continue their business conversation.

"Daman, I meant to tell you that my partners are attending the gala, as well as my parents and my grandfather. Vicky told me I could invite guests, so I'm assuming you were told the same thing."

"Yes. I invited my partners, my mom and James.

They continued talking about the gala, making sure that they were on the same page about everything that still needed to be done. Imani agreed with Daman's suggestion to leave for the gala in two days. Their family and friends would all arrive on the day of the event.

By the time their meals arrived, they were wrapping up their business conversation.

"The food here is delicious," Imani said after taking a couple bites.

Daman's gaze was fixated on her mouth, and she couldn't help but want to mess with him a little. She took another bite of her mashed potatoes, slowly licking the food off her fork. She saw his eyes darken, taking the bait.

"If you keep licking your fork like that, I won't show you any mercy tonight."

That was the first reference Daman had made to tonight, and she was glad to hear that his mind was fixated on the same thoughts as hers.

"Then I guess I need to keep licking my fork."

Seeing his eyes darken even more set her insides on fire. The moistness between her legs was making it hard for her to keep them closed, and she had to clamp them tighter to stop the developing ache. Daman started leaning into the table, and she followed his lead, leaning closer, as well.

"Imani, you're playing with fire. Don't you remember when we were in St. Simons Island? I didn't show you any mercy then, and I won't tonight, either."

*Hmmm...* Daman remembered the night a little differently than she had.

"Daman, there was a point during sex when I felt you pull back. Yes, you definitely fulfilled my desires that night, but I remember not showing you any mercy, either. Not even when I knew you wanted it."

Daman laughed a little louder than he'd probably meant to, but it wasn't loud or fast enough for Imani to miss the surprised look that initially crossed his face.

"Is that so? You didn't show me any mercy?"

"Nope. I didn't. I'm not ashamed to admit that you worked my body in ways I hadn't thought possible. But that doesn't mean I didn't notice that I had that same effect on you."

It seemed like minutes instead of seconds passed by without a word, only looks. Looks of promise, passion and even some looks that neither of them could explain. Her confidence was back. Imani felt it. It wasn't that her confidence had ever left, more like she'd been off balance. She knew Daman threw her off her game sometimes, but the minute she decided to be honest with herself and admit that she was interested in him, it became easier to truly speak her mind. The look on his face proved that she intrigued him by her honesty and that he was probably a little stunned she knew him so well.

"Don't think too much, Daman. I know I'm right."

He laughed another hearty laugh right before the waiter dropped off their check. After taking care of the bill, they promptly left the restaurant, ready to continue their night.

The entire car ride was filled with so much sexual tension that she didn't think they would ever make it back to her place. But Daman drove at record speed, quickly parking the car and hurrying them inside. The minute they stepped foot into her condo, he pulled her to him. She was surprised at how gently he kissed her, considering she felt like she was ready to explode. She'd always wanted to do something raunchy in her kitchen, and tonight was the perfect opportunity. She led Daman to her kitchen, their lips never breaking contact. When his back hit the counter, he twisted her around and lifted her onto the surface.

Daman briefly stopped kissing her as his hands went straight to the zipper of her dress.

"It's time to take this dress off," he said, even though his hands were already working the material off her.

She appreciated him taking his time so that he wouldn't rip the material, but she was impatient and needed to be naked with him.

His eyes lit up when he saw her spicy lingerie set. Within seconds, Daman discarded his clothes and threw them on the kitchen floor with her dress. She slowly lowered her hands onto his chest, thinking he could easily pass for a Ralph Lauren model for men's boxers. He placed one arm on either side of her, staring into her eyes as he let her rub her hands over his muscles, eventually returning to his chest and abs.

Daman grabbed her hands and lowered her back to the counter. He went to her freezer, grabbed a piece of ice, and placed it in between his lips before heading back toward her and removing her lingerie set. Seductively, he glided the ice across her body before dipping it into her wet center. The coldness from the ice combined with the heat of his tongue felt sensational. This was the first time someone tasted her with ice. The way he moved his tongue around her clitoris before sucking the ice into his mouth was gradually bringing her to her climax. Gripping his head, she rocked her hips to the motion of his cold tongue, releasing in an orgasm that overtook her whole body.

As her waves of passion subsided, Daman lifted her up to sit on the counter and placed soft kisses along her neck.

"That was nice," she said, knowing the comment didn't justify how she really felt.

He looked up at her and smiled. Staring back into his eyes, she felt it. It wasn't passion or lust. It was a feeling that was treading the thin line between *like* and *love*. If she were honest with herself, she'd admit her feelings for him ran deeper than she'd ever imagined. Her breath caught in her throat.

*That's what it is...I love him.*

A part of her wasn't surprised at all, since she'd been telling herself not to fall for him since they'd met. Her eyes darted across his face before taking in a deep breath and dropping her head to her chest. She didn't want him to see in her eyes what she felt in her heart. She sighed as thoughts began racing through her head.

*When did I fall for him? Was it in St. Simons Island?* She'd given up on those romantic dreams. She was a realist now, not an idealist. They'd only known each other for about three months.

*People don't fall in love that fast...* And yet, somehow, without realizing it, that's exactly what had happened to her. She'd thought she was doing a good job of keeping her heart guarded, but instead, she'd fallen in love with Daman Barker—a man who didn't believe in commitment or happily ever after.

Lifting her head and looking back up into his eyes, she decided she wouldn't tell him. She was the one who had fallen for him, knowing how the game was played, so it was her problem to deal with, not his. She wanted to make love to him, and their time together was limited. She no longer cared about what the future held. She only cared about enjoying him for as long as she could.

Leaning into him, she pulled his face closer to hers and kissed him with all the passion she felt. His response was instant, and slowly, his tongue started playing with hers. Leaning her on her back, he smoothly removed his boxers, hopped on the counter to join her and intimately began kissing her everywhere. Imani felt alive in every part of her body that his lips touched. His fingers dipped inside her center, finding her wet and ready. Slowly, his fingers began to twirl in a circular motion, exciting her so quickly that she could already feel the orgasm building inside her. His mouth connected with hers, and his kisses were filled with even more passion than they'd had before. She could feel the length of him on her thigh, increasing her level of desire.

"Daman, I want you inside me…now." She couldn't wait and needed to feel him.

"Who am I to disappoint?" Daman replied as he removed his fingers.

He looked down at his pants before getting off the counter to get a condom from his wallet. After the protection was in place, he kissed her again, and she welcomed the warmth of his tongue as it mated with hers. She'd never felt so vulnerable, yet she knew that with Daman, she didn't want it any other way. Being vulnerable would allow her to enjoy him in the fullest.

Slowly, she felt him push inside of her, his mouth leaving hers to watch her reaction as they connected in a way much stronger than the last. Once he was fully inside her, she watched a smile fill his face seconds before he began thrusting in and out of her. Her body knew his, and the only thought going through her mind as he thrust inside of her was that she wished she could enjoy this feeling forever. Her feelings were already involved, and she wasn't used to someone having so much control over her. If this happened to be the last time they made love, she wanted to show him how she felt. She wanted her body to say all the things that her voice couldn't say. Slightly pushing on his chest, she pushed herself up. At the look of confusion on Daman's face, she slowly pushed his back on the counter and climbed on top of him.

Luckily for her, Daman let her do what she wanted and helped ease her over his shaft. Once they were intimately connected again, she began to ride him with all the love she felt in her heart. She'd completely forgotten that she'd left her stereo on. It was the first time since they'd arrived back at her condo that she'd heard her Floetry CD playing in the background. She grinded her hips to the mellow music, letting go of all her inhibitions and putting her all into the one man who'd managed to get inside her heart. He had her hooked, and he had no idea how hard she'd fallen. If only for tonight, she'd milk the moment for all it was worth. She looked down at his face and was surprised to see him staring directly at her. Had he not been holding her hips in place, she probably would have hopped off the counter to avoid the force in his eyes.

Rotating her hips and balancing herself on her hands, she felt like they were doing more than making love. She saw something in his eyes but knew it couldn't be what she thought it was. Pushing her analytical views aside, she stopped trying to read Daman and instead increased her tempo so they could release the orgasms that were close to peaking.

Daman grabbed her hips and kept them planted as he met her thrust for thrust. Slowly, he began taking over, pushing them both to a higher level of ecstasy. Seconds later, they had orgasms so strong that Imani was glad Daman hadn't let her go yet. She screamed louder than she'd thought possible at the power the orgasm had over her. His growls indicated that he'd felt it, too. The joining of their bodies hadn't felt like one of lust. It had felt like so much more, but she didn't dare allow herself to believe he felt the same way about her as she did him. She crashed on top of his body, never recalling a time when she felt so alive and unrestrained. Tilting her head toward Daman, she knew the night had just begun for them.

"Are you ready to take this to the bedroom?"

Daman rubbed his hand through her hair and smiled back at her, making her heart skip a beat.

"Lead the way, baby."

Staring out the window of his Detroit condo, Daman tried to clear his mind of all the thoughts racing through his head. It was the day before he and Imani would arrive in Atlanta, and Daman was anxious.

He needed to take a warm shower to calm his mind. Showers always relieved his stress, and even though he knew he wouldn't completely forget about everything, he could try to ease the tension in his body. Stepping into the shower, his thoughts immediately went to Imani. He'd been thinking about her a lot lately, and it seemed like no matter what he did, she was never too far from his mind. They'd made love into the wee hours of the morning the other night, briefly stopping to eat something before continuing their sexual explorations. Any position he wanted to try, she was eager to try, as well. He'd felt more alive than ever, and the thought that he could have fallen for her scared him.

Right before they'd made love, he'd been staring into her eyes, and he saw it. He saw the exact moment when she realized that she'd fallen in love with him. At first, he didn't know what the look was that he saw in her eyes. When she dropped her head, he took the time to analyze the look he'd seen. He didn't recall ever seeing a woman look at him the way she did, and something inside him clicked. Something inside him knew that what he was seeing in her eyes was love. When she brought her head back up and met his eyes, he was certain that was what it was, and he could tell she was trying to hide it from him.

The crazy thing was that he knew he should have stopped what they were doing right then and there, put his clothes back on and gotten the hell out of there. Instead, even though the fact that she loved him scared him more than he'd like to admit, he didn't want to leave her. He couldn't leave her. Everything they'd done that night had felt like more than just feeding a hunger. There were unspoken promises in their lovemaking, and instead of running, Daman had embraced it.

*What happens now? How am I going to walk away from her in a few days?*

He couldn't allow himself to care so much for one

person. The world was unpredictable. *What if I lose her like I lost my dad?* More important, he knew that Imani deserved better, and he wasn't even sure if he could be the man she needed. Mr. Rayne had given him fair warning to leave Imani alone if he couldn't be the man she deserved. *But how am I supposed to give her up to another man when she's mine?*

He lifted up his head to let the water run over his face. *Mine? Why do I think she's mine?* The realization hit him hard on the head. She was his because he'd chosen her to be his, just as she'd chosen him to love. From the day he met her, he knew she wasn't the typical woman he went for. She was the type you married, and instead of steering clear, he did everything he could to draw her to him. In a way, he felt like he'd made her fall in love with him—probably because he had started falling in love with her before he knew what was happening to him. Imani couldn't belong to anyone else because he didn't want her to belong to anyone else. He'd forced her to open up to him and love him, and in turn he had opened up to her…and he loved her.

*Man, I love her…*

The words echoed in his mind, forcing him to come to terms with his feelings. When she wasn't around, all he did was miss her, and when she was around, all he wanted to do was keep her with him forever.

*Forever? Could I do forever?* There was a small voice inside of him that was saying *yes, you can do forever, as long as forever is with Imani.*

All his life he'd run from love, and quite frankly, he was tired of running. It was about time he listened to that voice inside him that told him to stop running. Imani was a proud and confident woman. There was no way he could say he loved her and not be prepared for her to be apprehensive. He knew she loved him, but he also knew that when he confessed his feelings, he needed to make it extra special. He needed to convince her that they weren't just in love…they had that forever kind of love.

## Chapter 20

The day of the First Annual Performance and Achievement Awards Gala had finally arrived, and it seemed everything was running smoothly, despite how busy the volunteers were. Daman had been running around all day finalizing everything on his to-do list. He knew Imani had called her partners and asked them to come a day early and work their magic for the pre-gala events and after party. Since everyone had been so busy, Daman had barely gotten a chance to see Imani. He missed her like crazy, and even though he would steal kisses from her every now and then, he wanted to be alone with her. The only time they'd been together was during a quick group meeting.

In an hour, the gala would begin, and people were already walking down the red carpet and being seated. It seemed everybody who's anybody had shown up to the awards gala, and he knew the team's hard work and dedication would pay off. He'd even seen the Simses, who'd expressed how proud they were of everyone's work. His mom and James had agreed.

Seeing Taheim and Jaleen, Daman quickly made his way over to them. "Glad to see you both got the backstage passes. Everyone else had already been here to see me, so I was hoping nothing was wrong."

Taheim looked at Jaleen before setting his eyes back on Daman.

"No, nothing was wrong. But we did come across something that we wanted to discuss with you. Is there anywhere private we could talk real quick?"

Daman could tell by the looks in his friends' eyes that it was serious, so he led them to a nearby office that he'd been using for the past couple of days.

"Okay, spill it. What do you need to talk to me about?"

Not wasting any time, Jaleen took out a manila envelope that he'd stuffed in the back of his tux. "We know what's going on with you. I was looking for a client folder and came across this envelope that you had locked in a drawer. I wasn't trying to snoop, but our keys all work for our file drawers, and I thought the file might be in there. We know about everything, D, and even though it seems like Malik has everything in order, we can't figure out why you didn't tell us about your uncle."

Daman stared at the men who were like brothers to him and knew he'd probably made the wrong decision by not telling them what was going on with Barker Architecture.

"I didn't want to worry you guys with my problems.

You allowed me to be a partner in the firm, and the last thing I wanted to do was give you a reason to regret your decision."

Taheim shook his head, disagreeing with what Daman was saying. "D, we're your boys. We made you a partner because you're good at what you do, and we have always dreamed of starting our own company together, even though we knew we still had to run our family businesses. You should have known you could trust us."

"And we can worry about ourselves," Jaleen added. "We're a team, so when one of us is in trouble, we all step up and handle it together."

Looking at his friends, Daman knew he was lucky. Not many men would have read everything that was in that file and still trust him as they did.

"There were some things I went along with that I'm not proud of. I should have questioned him more. After my father died, I looked up to my uncle so it was hard to think he was capable of embezzling money."

Jaleen and Taheim nodded their heads in understanding.

"Malik was able to gather enough evidence against my uncle for me to turn him in. Fortunately, I didn't even need to do that. My uncle met with me and told me everything…he explained why he did it. Why he felt he couldn't stop embezzling money. Yesterday, I went with him to turn himself in. I still have a lot I need to work out so I'm going to get our lawyers and executive team together to come up with a plan."

"That's good, D," Taheim said as the three men walked back out of the office.

"Have you told Imani?" Jaleen asked.

"We talked about my uncle, but she doesn't know the details. I plan on telling her soon, though."

Right after he answered, he heard Imani's laugh and turned to see her, her parents, grandfather and partners headed in their direction.

"And since I'm being honest with you guys now, yes, something more is going on between us."

Imani looked stunning in her navy blue evening gown. She'd changed out of her pre-gala dress, and he'd never seen her look more gorgeous.

"That beautiful woman coming toward us, gentlemen, is the woman I love and the future Mrs. Barker. She just doesn't know it yet."

Both Taheim and Jaleen shared a laugh, each slapping Daman on the back.

"Your secret's safe with us, man," Jaleen responded before Imani and the group made it to them.

Everyone exchanged hugs and continued saying what a great job the volunteer team had done to pull off such a huge event. Daman pulled Imani aside to make sure everything on her end of the planning was going smoothly.

They only had forty minutes before the gala was going to start and Daman had a few other things he needed to accomplish beforehand. He pulled Mr. Burrstone aside to get confirmation from him that it was okay to go forth with his plan. Daman really respected Mr. Burrstone so he'd called him yesterday to tell him what he planned to do.

"I think it's time, son," Ed said, clasping Daman's shoulders.

"Can I have everyone's attention," Daman said to his partners, Imani's parents and her partners. "Can you all follow me, please? I only need ten minutes of your time."

"Daman, what's this about?" Imani asked.

Daman walked over to her and grabbed her arm. "Just follow me," he said as he led her down the hall with everyone following behind. He stopped at a conference room and walked inside. As discussed, his mother was sitting in the room awaiting their arrival.

"Hello, Mrs. Barker," Imani said, giving her a soft hug.

"Hello, sweetie," Patricia replied as she returned the hug.

Daman made introductions before asking everyone to sit at the table.

"I know you all are wondering why I asked you to meet in here before the gala," Daman said to the group. "I recently learned some information a couple days ago and felt like now was the perfect time to disclose this information. Secrets tend to destroy relationships and since this secret affects Imani and myself, I felt it best to reveal the secret in front of the people we love most."

The look of confusion was evident on Imani's face.

"Mom, you want to take the lead?"

"Okay, son," Patricia said as she stood to talk.

"When my husband, Stan, died, I was devastated. It took me a long time to accept the fact that although my husband was gone, that didn't mean I had to stop living my life. I pushed away so many people I loved and broke so many great friendships, that I didn't know how to mend the bonds I'd broken. That includes my friendship with Edward and Faith Burrstone."

Imani gasped, clearly surprised by the news. So were her partners and Daman's partners. But Imani's parents only smiled, leading Daman to believe they'd known all along.

Patricia glanced at Imani. "I should have told you, too, Imani. You are so much like your grandmother that it felt like I was seeing a ghost when you came to my house."

"And Daman," Patricia said as she turned to Daman. "I should have told you that I knew Imani as soon as you got to my house. I just couldn't deal with you being disappointed in me. I'd turned away from so many people who tried to help me get over your father."

"Mom, you don't owe me an apology," Daman responded as he pulled his mom into a hug. "I know what you went through when we lost Dad."

Patricia sobbed as Daman consoled her. "Yes, I do," Patricia said, breaking their hug and walking over to Ed.

"Faith tried to be there for me so many times," Patricia said to Ed. "I am so sorry I let the despair I was feeling from losing Stan affect my relationship with Faith. I exiled all my friends and family from my life, but she was the only one who continued to be there for me. I received every Christmas and birthday card that she ever sent me, but I was too embarrassed to ask for forgiveness. So on behalf of Faith, I'll ask for your forgiveness, instead."

Ed draped his arms over Patricia and pulled her into a hug.

"Patricia, Faith knew you loved her, and she knew one day you'd realize that you have friends and family who love you and want to be there for you. Ever since Stan's death, you haven't really been living your life. We're getting old, woman. Now, don't you think it's time to start living again?"

Laughing, Patricia playfully slapped Ed on the arm. "I think that sounds like a great idea."

Yesterday, when Daman had talked to Ed, he'd told him that Uncle Frank was always jealous of the closeness Stan and he shared. When he heard Barker Architecture was in trouble, he wanted to help, but figured Frank wouldn't be receptive, so he used a fake name.

Daman looked over at Imani and saw her dabbing tears out of her eyes. She stared back at him with that adorable look he loved so much. He was glad to see the love still shining in her eyes. After all this drama, the only thing he could think about doing was taking her back to his hotel room and locking themselves away from the outside world for a couple of days. She winked at him and smiled a smile that promised in due time, she'd make his wish come true.

The gala was a huge success, and Imani was glad that everything had gone perfectly. Business owners and entrepreneurs from around the United States were present and men and women came dressed to impress. A lot of awards were given out to individual entrepreneurs and business owners, but the awards that received the most media buzz were the businesses that won the lifetime achievement, excellent community service and outstanding performance awards. Imani was eager to see what new technology product would develop from the tech company that won the award for having the best innovative ideas and products.

Black Enterprise was extremely pleased with the way everything turned out and thanked Imani and Daman at the end of the ceremony. Attendees were requesting her business card left and right when they found out Elite Events helped plan the amazing event. She and her partners had to get a game plan together as soon as they got back to Chicago.

Making her way to the room where the after party was taking place, she couldn't help but reflect on the revelations that were disclosed earlier. Imani still couldn't believe their families knew each other!

During the conversation between her grandfather and Patricia, Cyd had whispered to Imani to look at their parents' reactions. One look and she knew that the Barkers and the Burrstones had been longtime friends. She'd gotten a chance to talk to Patricia and her mom a few minutes before the gala began. Patricia confessed that most of the furniture in her home was made up of pieces she and Gamine found together. On one of those shopping days, Imani and Daman had actually been with them. The picture of her and Gamine that sat over her fireplace was taken by Daman's mom outside of one of the stores. To think that she and Daman had actually met before baffled her, but it was comforting at the same time.

Closing her eyes, she remembered a time when she went shopping with Gamine and became friends with the son of one of Gamine's friends. Back then, boys were disgusting, and she didn't initially want to play with him. But he convinced her to play hide-and-seek outside the furniture store, and they'd had so much fun that she'd made Gamine promise to bring her back to play with him again.

During the entire story, Hope had been smiling at Imani. Her mom confessed that Ed had decided to tell her and her father everything a couple weeks ago but made them promise not to say anything and to let everything work out on its own. She knew she loved Daman, and knowing about his relationship with his uncle and his struggle to right a wrong only made her love him more. She wanted a future with him. She wanted her fairy-tale ending. But he didn't love her; he only lusted after her, and in her book, that was a big difference.

During intermission, she told Daman the story Patricia had told her about them meeting before. He just smiled, kissed her and told her that they had to get the show on the road. She hoped that hadn't meant that he was already trying to figure out how he would let her down gently. He probably figured that since their families seemed to have rekindled a friendship, he needed to break this thing off fast before he hurt her. Newsflash, Daman: her heart was already in it, and later, she planned on telling him just that.

Walking into the room where the after party was being held, she was surprised to see her family and friends there. Daman had told her to arrive thirty minutes before the party started to make sure everything was set up properly. No one had noticed she'd entered the room until the door shut behind her, causing everyone to turn around.

"Why are you all in here already?"

"They're here because I asked them to be," Daman said as he emerged from behind her.

"I realized that almost everyone in this room has had a hand in getting us together."

She didn't dare hope he was doing what she wished he was doing, so she let him continue without asking another question.

"Since meeting you, my entire life has changed for the better. When my father died, I swore I would never allow myself to love someone so hard, only to have that person taken away from me. I knew the minute you walked into the Simses' office, you were unlike any woman I'd ever met. Over the course of our partnership, I completely forgot we were vying for the same estate. I don't know exactly when I fell in love with you because if I think about it, I can't remember a time in these past few months when I wasn't in love with you. When we were younger and Gamine and my mom took us shopping, I remember playing outside with you and having the time of my life. I told my mom that for a girl, you were okay, and I wouldn't mind playing with you again. I didn't realize many years later, that same little girl would be the woman I'd want to spend the rest of my life with. You make me want to strive to be a better man, and I've found myself opening up to you in ways that I've never opened up with anyone else. I think both of us had our hearts guarded when we first met. But somewhere along the way, you broke the guard around my heart. I would love nothing more than for you to make me the happiest man in the world and be my wife."

Bending down on one knee, Daman pulled out the

most beautiful ring she'd ever seen. She couldn't stop the tears from falling as she got lost in his eyes.

"Imani Rayne, will you marry me?"

Wiping the tears off her face, she tried her best to control all the emotions she was feeling.

"When I first met you, I thought you were arrogant and sarcastic. I thought you saw yourself as God's gift to women." Hearing Taheim and Jaleen laugh behind them caused her to smile.

"But I was wrong to judge you. The more I got to know you, the more I learned about the true Daman Barker…the man behind the sarcastic comments and arrogant ways. Being a proud man doesn't make you arrogant, and your sarcasm was just a part of your sense of humor. I think I've slowly been falling in love with you since the day we met, even though I've tried to keep myself from doing just that. I'd forgotten that we were supposed to be vying for the estate, too. I do remember that time playing when we were younger, and I also remember making Gamine promise to take me to play with you again one day. Your strength and determination are only a few qualities of yours that have made me fall deeper in love with you."

Talking a little softer, Imani continued. "I admire the man that you are so much, and I can't imagine spending the rest of my life with anyone else. Yes, Daman Barker, I will marry you because I want nothing more than to be your wife."

As Daman slid the ring on her finger, he looked into her eyes, and Imani saw the love that he had for her. He also handed her a paper that showed the Simses had released both properties to the future Mr. and Mrs.

Daman Barker, on the condition that they could only get the properties as husband and wife. All of their family and friends were clapping and cheering for them, but as his lips got closer to hers, all she could think about was how happy she was to be sharing her life with such an amazing man.

As soon as his lips touched hers, she felt the butterflies in her stomach and welcomed the feelings and emotions she used to try to hide. Daman had taught her to let go of the past and focus on the present, when he had actually been a part of her past. They had been the missing piece in each other's puzzle. They had been missing that piece of their past *and* their present lives. But now, sharing this kiss with Daman, she couldn't think of the past or the present…only a future with the man who'd stolen her heart.

# *Epilogue*

Imani stared out the bedroom window on the top floor
of her grandfather's house, and couldn't help but smile
at how wonderful all the decorations in the backyard
looked. The landscape was already beautiful, but the
elegant decorations that had been added took her breath
away.

Elite Events Incorporated had managed to pull off
the wedding of the year in only two months. She knew
that Cyd, Lex, Mya and the team were overwhelmed
with how quickly they had to pull everything together,
but after all, it was her wedding, and she wanted the
day to be perfect. Luckily, she had friends and family who loved her so much that they were willing to
dedicate their time to make sure everything went off
without a hitch.

Frank's trial was starting soon, and Daman had
insisted that they get married before it began. They

were lucky enough to be blessed with a seventy-degree October day, and Imani couldn't be happier.

"Sis, I know it's your big day and you're entitled to do what you want, but if we don't get you in this wedding dress, Mom and Mrs. Barker are going to hurt us. The wedding is already running behind schedule."

She laughed at Cyd's comment because her bridesmaids were all in their lavender dresses, yet she and Daman had shown up late for their own wedding. Traditionally, the bride and groom were not supposed to see each other the night before the big day. Daman figured that getting a quickie in on the day of the wedding didn't count. When he showed up at her condo at 12:01 a.m., she didn't have the heart to tell him that his version of "tradition" was wrong.

"We know what you're thinking about," Mya said. "And don't think we couldn't hear what you were doing in your bedroom. We were right down the hall."

"And Aunt Hope would seriously kill us if she knew we let you and Daman fool around the morning of your wedding," Lex added. "We were supposed to be there to make sure that didn't happen."

Imani didn't care. She was glad he'd stopped over. They'd been doing so much planning that they'd barely gotten a chance to see each other.

Cyd cleared her throat, causing Imani to glance over at her. Lately, Cyd had seemed bothered by something, and Imani wished she knew what it was. She'd asked her several times while they were planning the wedding, and each time, Cyd said she was fine. But she knew better. Something was bothering Cyd, and after her honeymoon, she'd have to focus on getting Cyd to talk about whatever was troubling her.

A knock at the door interrupted her thoughts.

"Oh, no," Lex said, as she went over to answer the door. She assumed it was Hope or one of the aunts. Instead, all the women were surprised to see Mrs. Sims.

"Imani, you don't have on your dress yet!" Mrs. Sims said in surprise. Imani got up to hug the woman who held a special place in her heart.

"No, but I was just about to put it on."

"Well, now you can wait," Mrs. Sims replied before turning toward the bridesmaids. "Ladies, can we have a minute?"

"Sure," Cyd answered, as she ushered everyone out of the room.

"Imani, sweetie, I have something to share with you," Mrs. Sims said. "By now, you know that I had the pleasure of watching both you and Daman grow up. Through your union, Patricia and I have reconnected, and I'm so happy that you and Daman are getting married."

Imani watched as Mrs. Sims pulled out an envelope with her name on it.

"Sweetie, Gamine asked me to give you this letter on your wedding day. I would explain more, but it is my understanding that this letter will explain it all."

Imani couldn't slow the beating of her heart. Her eyes instantly filled with tears at how monumental the moment was. She'd wished every night that Gamine could be at her wedding, and now, she had a letter that was written to her to read on her wedding day. Mrs. Sims kissed her cheek before heading toward the door.

Opening the handwritten letter, she quickly steadied her shaking hands and began reading.

*My Dearest Imani,*

*Of all my grandchildren, you were always the nurturer—the one who would try her best to make sure everyone was okay and getting along. Your heart loves to its fullest, and you are so giving that I hope you make sure to give a little to your-self, too. I know today is your wedding day, and more than anything I wish I were there for you. I know the grandkids never liked my meddling, but in this case, I think you'll forgive me. I thank Da-man's father, Stan, for making his son believe the estate was something he should go after because I did the same thing for you. Of course, Stan and I always thought we'd be around to see the love story unfold, but everything happens for a rea-son. We knew that when the time was right and the Simses decided to sell, you both would try to fulfill our wishes. And I'm forever grateful to the Simses, as well as Vicky and Pete for fulfilling my wishes, as crazy as I knew they were. Baby, you and Daman were meant for each other. This was the only way I could think of to get you both to-gether. Don't ask me how I knew you two would eventually fall in love. A grandmother just knows these things. I asked Mrs. Sims to withhold this letter if either of you had found love elsewhere, so if you're reading this, that means fate has played a hand, as well. Enjoy the estate because it does hold the answers you and Daman were search-*

*ing for...a fulfilling life with the one person you can't live without. There will be good times and bad times, as there are in every marriage. Always remember to cherish the good times, and never forget that together, you can overcome any obstacle. I may have left this earth, but I will forever be in your heart. It was my time to go, and now my dear Imani...it is your time to live...*
*With all the love in my heart,*
*Gamine*

The tears running down Imani's face weren't sad tears but tears of happiness. In more ways than one, Gamine had filled an emptiness she'd felt in her heart and answered a lot of questions that she and Daman had after they thought about their journey to finding each other. She hid the letter in her purse as she heard the door open and saw the concerned looks on her bridesmaids' faces.

"I'll be fine, ladies, don't worry."

Cyd was staring at her the hardest, and she knew none of the women believed her.

"Come on, seriously. Are you all going to stand there and look at me or help me get ready? I'm dying to marry that man down there, but I can't get married looking like this."

All four women laughed and started working.

Imani leaned over and kissed Daman as they shared their first dance as husband and wife. The wedding had been everything they'd hoped for, packed with friends and family from all over the country. Breaking off the kiss, she couldn't help but laugh at the irritated look on Daman's face.

"Woman, you will not be breaking kisses with me anytime you please. As your husband, I can kiss you for as long as I want, anytime I want."

Tilting her head, she tried to figure out what she could say to make him see reason.

"Baby, I know that, but everyone is watching us, and I can feel you getting excited."

Daman shrugged and glanced around the room. "I don't care."

Laughing again, Imani decided to give in and continue kissing her husband. She heard a few catcalls from the women and chants from the men as their kiss deepened. Imani felt something slowly brush her cheek and lifted her head to see what it was. Glancing down, she saw a beautiful white feather that was almost unnoticeable because it blended with her dress. She looked at Daman and saw that he noticed it, too. Picking up the feather, Daman placed it behind her ear before they continued their dance.

Glancing around the room at her cousins, she noticed that they had seen the feather, too. She saw Mya hug Cyd and Lex as each woman dabbed their eyes. She knew then that none of them had tossed the feather, which could only mean one thing—Gamine was looking down on them.

"I think Gamine is trying to tell you something," Daman whispered in Imani's ear. She had shared the contents of the letter with him, and they agreed it would be their secret for now.

"I think she is, too, and I got the message loud and clear."

\* \* \* \* \*

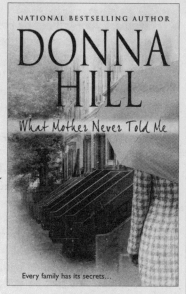

# REQUEST YOUR FREE BOOKS!

## 2 FREE NOVELS
## PLUS 2 FREE GIFTS!

KIMANI
ROMANCE ™

### Love's ultimate destination!

## New York Times **Bestselling Author**

# BRENDA JACKSON

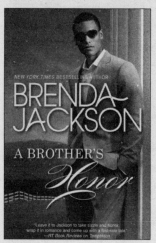

*The Granger brothers left behind their family's Virginia estate—and the bad memories it holds—years ago. But their dying grandfather's request to make things right has brought them home…*

As the eldest brother, attorney Jace Granger is determined to take responsibility for his family's failing business. As CEO, he hires a consultant to turn the company around. Smart, sexy Shana Bradford is the right person for the job—and the right woman to turn Jace's world upside down.

But old secrets begin to emerge. A woman from Jace's past suddenly reappears. And an explosive discovery changes everything Jace thinks he knows about his mother—and his father, who was convicted of her murder.

Jace soon learns he needs to face the past…or risk losing his future.

## **Available wherever books are sold.**

**Be sure to connect with us at:**
Harlequin.com/Newsletters
Facebook.com/HarlequinBooks
Twitter.com/HarlequinBooks

**HARLEQUIN**® MIRA®
www.Harlequin.com

MBJ1433